# Kneel for Mercy

## Barbara Cartland

BANTAM BOOKS
TORONTO · NEW YORK · LONDON · SYDNEY

KNEEL FOR MERCY

*A Bantam Book / July 1982*

ISBN 0-553-22712-2

*Published simultaneously in the United States and Canada*

---

*Bantam Books are published by Bantam Books, Inc. Its trademark,*
*consisting of the words "Bantam Books" and the portrayal of a*
*rooster, is Registered in U.S. Patent and Trademark Office and in*
*other countries. Marca Registrada. Bantam Books, Inc., 666 Fifth*
*Avenue, New York, New York 10103.*

---

PRINTED IN THE UNITED STATES OF AMERICA

0  9  8  7  6  5  4  3  2  1

# Author's Note

Smuggling during the Napoleonic War accelerated what was already a national business. At the end of the century, gangs had terrorised the South Coast in an "open war" between smugglers and Customs men.

At the time of this story, smugglers were the "friends" of Napoleon Bonaparte and they were allowed to build their galleys in Calais, which were banned in England. The Emperor himself said that there were upwards of five hundred English smugglers in Dunkirk alone.

The transfer of gold to guineas to pay for the large cargoes bought in France and Holland was estimated to reach between ten thousand and twelve thousand guineas per week.

Smugglers also carried war secrets and French spies across the Channel. The notorious smuggler Jack Rattenburg was caught, and it was found that he had agreed to bring four French Officers to England for one hundred pounds.

# Chapter One

## 1814

Marista carried the eggs that Hannah had cooked from the kitchen into the small Dining-Room and put them down on the table.

As she did so, she glanced at the clock and hoped that Letty would not be late.

Her sister liked reading late into the night and therefore was usually late for breakfast, which distressed Marista because eggs were precious, and if they were cold when Letty came downstairs she invariably left them untouched.

But that morning her fears were groundless, for she heard the sound of footsteps, the door opened, and Letty came hurrying into the room.

"Good-morning, dearest!" she said to her sister. "I am as hungry as a hunter!"

"The hens have been obliging, for a change," Marista answered, "so eat your eggs while they are hot."

"I have every intention of doing so," Letty replied.

She sat down at the table with her back to the window, and as the sunshine made a halo of her hair, Marista thought that no-one could look more lovely and it was a pity there was nobody of any importance to see her.

1

Every day it seemed to her that Letty, who had been christened "Lettice," grew more attractive and more beautiful, and she thought that if their mother were alive and they were living at the Castle, invitations would be pouring in for Balls, Receptions, and parties of every description.

As it was, nobody bothered about two unimportant girls living in a small house on the Estate which was no longer theirs.

Days and sometimes weeks went by without their seeing anybody but old Hannah and the people in the village.

But it was no use regretting the past, Marista thought, and they just had to make the best of the present.

Letty ate her eggs, then said with a note of excitement in her voice:

"What do you think, Marista? More vans arrived at the Castle yesterday, and I could see furniture being carried in and also what looked like paintings in cases."

Marista's lips tightened for a moment. Then she said:

"I have told you before, Letty, we must not peep and pry. The Castle has nothing to do with us."

"I know that," Letty replied, "but nevertheless, it is exciting. Do you think the Earl is coming here himself?"

There was a pause before Marista replied:

"Hannah was told that he . . . arrived last night."

Letty gave a little cry.

"I do not believe it! How thrilling! Perhaps he will give parties, and although we will not be asked to them, at least we might see his guests arriving."

"I have no wish to have anything to do with the Earl of Stanbrook," Marista said coldly.

The way she spoke made her sister look at her sharply. Then Letty replied:

2

"Of course I understand what you are feeling, dearest, and I feel the same. He is a horrible, odious creature, and if we ever meet him we will tell him so. At the same time, anything unusual is an excitement here."

As that was undoubtedly true, Marista had no answer. She merely buttered sparingly a piece of toast and spread it with crab-apple jam which she and Hannah had made last autumn from the apples off the tree in their own garden.

As she did so, she knew that the trees at the Castle were laden with unpicked fruit, and in the greenhouses, although they needed repairing, peaches and grapes were ripening until they rotted.

Then she thought of the Castle itself, shuttered and barred.

It was, she thought every time she looked at it, a bitter memorial to her father's foolishness, and it made her want to cry.

Letty interrupted her thoughts by saying pensively:

"I wonder what he is really like."

"Who?"

"The Earl, of course. Because of what happened to Papa, we have always thought of him as an Ogre, a monster who has gobbled up our happiness, and therefore we have cringed from him in horror."

She spoke so dramatically that Marista could not help laughing.

"I do not think anybody can be as bad as that," she said in her soft voice. "At the same time, it is impossible for us not to hate the Earl."

"Of course he is loathsome," Letty agreed, "and I suppose he did not cheat in the game he played with Papa, although we would like to think he did."

"I am sure he would not do that," Marista agreed. "After all, Letty, he is a gentleman and a sportsman. At the same time . . ."

3

She paused.

"Go on!" Letty prompted.

"It is no use talking about it," Marista said hastily. "What is done cannot be undone."

Letty put her arms on the table and rested her lovely face on her hands.

"Looking back," she said, "I suppose I was too young at the time to understand exactly what happened, but I cannot help thinking that it was extremely foolish of Papa to think that gaming when he could not afford it was the only way to pay a debt."

"What else could he do?" Marista asked. "Actually, Mama said the same thing, but it was too late to stop him."

Letty smiled.

"Papa was impulsive and I am the same. You are more like Mama."

"I hope so," Marista answered. "I would be very flattered if I were only a tiny bit like her."

"You are very like her," Letty insisted. "The people in the village are always saying: 'Miss Marista be just like her mother, God rest her, one of th' kindest an' loveliest ladies as ever walked this earth!' "

She mimicked the way the village people talked, and Marista laughed.

"It is a good thing somebody appreciates us."

There was silence for a moment. Then Letty asked:

"Just suppose . . . the Earl did ask us to a party would . . . you go?"

"Certainly not!" Marista replied. "I wish to have nothing to do with him. Do not forget that he is the reason why poor Anthony is having to work for Farmer Dawson, and hating every moment of it."

"At least he earns some money," Letty said. "I lay awake last night trying to think if there was any way in which you and I could make some. There must be something we could do, Marista."

"I have thought and thought," Marista replied. "But despite the very good education Mama insisted we should have, it is very humiliating to think that unless we scrub doorsteps or become milk-maids there is no chance of our earning a single penny!"

Then in a very different tone of voice she said:

"Talking of milk-maids, it is your turn to fetch the milk from the farm, and you will find the money for what we have had this week on the dresser in the kitchen."

Letty gave a sigh.

"That means I shall have to listen to Mother Johnson moaning on about the 'old days' and saying how the war has taken all the best and strongest men from the land, and there is nobody to mend the farmhouse roof, which lets in the rain."

"I have heard it too," Marista said. "I am sorry for the Johnsons. They are growing too old to farm such a large acreage, with both their sons away fighting Napoleon, and the only help they have left is a man of sixty, and he is the village idiot."

"Looney Ben is certainly no good for anything," Letty remarked.

"He feeds the chickens and finds the eggs," Marista replied, "and even his pair of hands are better than none."

"He is always hanging about," Letty remarked. "He gives me the creeps!"

"Just hurry to the farm and back again," Marista said. "If you tell Mrs. Johnson that Hannah wants the milk for luncheon, she will not be able to detain you."

Letty made a little grimace but did not answer, and at that moment Hannah came into the room.

"There's a letter for you, Miss Marista," she said. "It must have been pushed through the door last night or early this morning. I've only just found it."

"A letter?"

5

Hannah lifted the envelope up to her eyes. Then she exclaimed:

"I see now it's addressed to your mother. '*Lady Rockbourne*' is what's written on it, but there's no address."

"I wonder who it can be from," Marista said. "Obviously a stranger, not to know that Mama has been . . . dead for . . . over a . . . year."

There was a little throb in her voice, for even now it was hard to speak of her mother without knowing how much she missed her.

"Well, all I hopes," Hannah said, "is that it's not a bill. There's too many of them as it is."

"Do we owe very much?" Marista asked in a frightened voice.

"Enough to start me worrying," Hannah replied, "an' I've told Master Anthony to give me more out of his wages than he did last week. He seems to think I can feed him on air!"

As she finished speaking, Hannah picked up the empty dish which had contained the eggs and left the Dining-Room.

Letty laughed.

"Anthony is always complaining that Hannah takes every penny he earns, and he said last Friday that if he had to keep a woman he would rather she were younger and more attractive!"

"Letty!" Marista exclaimed in a shocked voice. "How can you say such things?"

"It is what Anthony said, and of course at his age it is natural that he should want to take out a 'Bit o' Muslin,' or one of those dancers from Covent Garden, who he says are so alluring that no gentleman can resist them."

Marista looked even more shocked. Then she said almost as if she were speaking to herself:

"Those are things that Anthony certainly cannot . . . afford to do."

Letty parted her lips as if she had a retort to make, then changed her mind.

Instead, she watched as her sister opened the note which Hannah had given her, and she knew that Marista was apprehensive as to what it contained.

She pulled out a thin sheet of writing-paper, stared at it for a moment, then gave an exclamation of horror.

"What is it? What have you read?" Letty asked.

"I cannot . . . believe . . . it!" Marista faltered.

She looked at the writing-paper she held in her hand, and her sister saw that she was trembling.

"There . . . must be some . . . mistake."

Without saying any more, Marista passed the writing-paper to Letty, who read aloud:

*My Lady:*

*On the orders of the Earl of Stanbrook, owner of Rock Castle Estate, I have been empowered to collect the rents from his tenants.*

*It has come to my notice that during the two-and-a-half years you have occupied your present premises, known as 'Dovecot House,' His Lordship has received no rent.*

*Taking everything into account, it is estimated that a fair rent for the house, garden, and two paddocks would be one hundred pounds per year.*

*I would therefore be obliged if Your Ladyship would arrange for the sum of two hundred fifty pounds to be brought to the Estate Office as soon as possible.*

*I remain, My Lady,*
*Your most humble and respectful*
*servant,*
*Emmanual Robertson.*

As Letty finished speaking she stared at the letter in the same way that Marista had, as if she could not believe what she had read.

Then she looked at her sister with an expression of fear in her eyes.

"Two hundred fifty pounds!" she exclaimed. "How can we possibly find such a large sum of money?"

"It is impossible," Marista said, "as you well know! Oh, Letty, Letty, how can this have happened to us? I thought that Papa had arranged when we moved out of the Castle for us to live here . . . free."

"I believed it was our house," Letty said. "It never struck me for one moment that we could be turned away like beggars."

Marista did not reply. She merely put her hands up to her eyes.

They had felt safe at Dovecot House after everything had fallen in ruins about them.

When their father had returned from London to tell them he had lost the Castle and the Estate that had been in the Rockbourne family for three hundred years, at first it had been impossible to understand what he was saying.

Yet, they had to face the truth that while they had been poor before, they were now practically penniless.

Sir Richard Rockbourne, Baronet, had always been excessively proud of his heritage, his ancient Castle, and his ancestry, which went back to the reign of Henry VIII.

James II had dubbed the Rockbourne of the day—a respected Statesman—a Baronet, and thereafter each head of the family had passed on the title and the Castle to his son.

However, they had grown poorer in the passing years, but they still remained excessively proud.

Because he was handsome and dashing and enjoyed

life to the fullest, it was understandable that Sir Richard lived beyond his means.

When he married for love the beautiful daughter of a neighbouring Squire who unfortunately had two sons to provide for, the Rockbourne relations had shaken their heads.

They had said somewhat acidly that the only chance Sir Richard had of saving the Castle was to seek a wife who had a large dowry.

However, he had pleased himself, as he had done since the cradle, and was blissfully happy with his wife to the point where they seldom went to London but were quite content to live in the country.

There they rode their well-bred horses, Sir Richard shot over his broad acres, and they entertained a wide circle of friends without troubling themselves particularly over the cost of such hospitality.

It was only when the creditors became more and more pressing that Sir Richard realised he must do something about it, and, as Letty had said, he had impulsively gone off to London, determined to make a fortune at gaming.

In the past he had been on the whole a very successful player at the gaming-tables.

Unfortunately and tragically, he had on this occasion encountered the Earl of Stanbrook.

The Earl, because of his successes on the Turf, was well known the length and breadth of the country, and he was cheered on every race-course where his horses passed the winning-post first with almost monotonous regularity.

It was inevitable that he should also be a close friend and confidant of the Prince of Wales, who had now become Prince Regent, and who was called somewhat mockingly "The Prince of Pleasure."

Marista and Anthony, as the two elder children,

could not help learning a great deal about the Earl from hearing their father talk about him to their mother, although Letty was fortunately too young to understand the implications of much that was said.

"I see Stanbrook won the two thousand guineas at Newmarket," their father would say at the breakfast-table when he looked at the newspapers. "That man is so lucky that there is something uncanny about it. In fact, somebody was saying last week that he had sold his soul to the Devil!"

Lady Rockbourne had given a little cry of protest.

"That, darling, is a very cruel thing to say about anybody!"

"I am not certain it is not true," Sir Richard said lightly. "Just look at his record: he wins every race, he has all the Beauties of London fluttering round him like moths round a candle, he owns the finest horses and the largest Estates, and naturally he has under his protection the most alluring Cyprians any man could imagine."

"Oh, Richard! Not in front of the children!" Lady Rockbourne had said quickly.

"You forget, Mama," Anthony interrupted, "that Marista and I are grown up, and if she does not know what a Cyprian is, I do, and Papa is talking sense. I saw Stanbrook with one the other day. She was the most exquisite creature one could ever imagine and was glittering with diamonds like a Christmas-Tree!"

"I do not wish to hear about such women!" Lady Rockbourne said quickly. "And neither Marista nor Letty should know that such creatures exist."

"They are not likely to come in contact with them," Anthony said, "nor am I, for that matter, while my pockets are to let."

"A very good thing, too," his mother replied.

She then took the girls from the Dining-Room, and

only when the door was shut behind them did Anthony look at his father with a grin and say:

"You have shocked Mama."

"I know," Sir Richard replied, "and I must apologise to her. I spoke without thinking, but Stanbrook gets under my skin."

"I suppose we are all jealous of him," Anthony said. "Somebody was saying in London last week that he is the best shot they have ever seen, and when he fights a duel he draws blood exactly in the place he wishes, and fires so quickly that his opponent does not have a chance!"

"I have no wish to fight a duel with anybody," Sir Richard remarked. "At the same time, I am human enough to hope that Stanbrook has an Achilles' heel somewhere."

"You need not waste your time looking, Papa," Anthony said, laughing. "If he had one, or a heart, some woman would have found it by now. The gossips say he has never been in love and discards women as soon as they bore him, as another man would throw away a pair of worn gloves."

"I am sick of talking about him," Sir Richard said, rising from the table. "Come and have a look at the new horse I bought yesterday. He was expensive, but I think he was worth the money I paid for him."

Unfortunately, cheap or expensive, the horse was not paid for at the time, nor were a number of others.

There were also Phaetons, pieces of furniture, paintings, and other items which had taken Sir Richard's fancy and had been brought to the Castle on credit.

When finally the day of reckoning arrived, he was appalled and astounded that he could owe so much.

"How could I have been so extravagant?" he asked his wife.

"No one thing has been very expensive," Lady

Rockbourne said miserably, "it is just that when it is all added up together, it comes to an astronomical sum."

She sounded so unhappy that Sir Richard put his arms round her and drew her close to him.

"I will not have you worrying," he said. "I will meet my debts somehow, although God knows I have no idea at the moment how it can be done."

"Perhaps we . . . could sell . . . something," Lady Rockbourne suggested weakly.

"If you are thinking of the paintings or of anything else in the Castle, the answer is 'no'!" her husband said with a hard note in his voice. "However hard-up my father was, he kept everything intact for me, and I intend to do the same for Anthony."

"But, darling, we do not own anything except the Castle and the Estate."

"I know," Sir Richard answered, "but I will find a way. Do not worry."

She had worried, but she knew her husband would not wish her to interfere, and when Sir Richard said he was going to London she did not protest.

However, there were some empty stalls in the stables, and he also borrowed money from one of their neighbours who was a close friend.

Only when he was actually leaving did he say insistently:

"Pray for me, my darling, that I shall be able to come back to you with my head held high and no longer feeling apprehensive whenever there is a knock at the door."

"Oh, Richard, what are you going to do?" his wife asked.

"Make a fortune, my precious. When I bring it back to you, you shall have the most beautiful gown in England that I can buy."

"Suppose you fail?" Lady Rockbourne asked in a whisper.

"I never fail," Sir Richard boasted. "I have been lucky all my life, but never more lucky than when you said you would marry me. I love you, my darling, and I intend to keep you in the comfort to which you are accustomed."

He had kissed her, then had driven away looking amazingly handsome and somewhat raffish with his high hat on the side of his dark hair, which as yet had not a single strand of grey in it.

Marista had waved him good-bye, then as his Phaeton drawn by four horses disappeared down the drive, she became aware that her mother was crying.

"What is the matter, Mama?" she asked in surprise.

"Your father is so brave and so optimistic," Lady Rockbourne replied, "but I am a coward, Marista, and I am afraid he will fail."

Marista thought afterwards that her mother must have had a presentiment of what the future would bring.

Four days later, her father had returned looking very different from the smiling, dashing man who had left them.

He seemed years older, and there was a hollow look about his eyes which was somehow frightening.

There was no need for him to tell them that he had not won.

"What has happened?" Lady Rockbourne had asked when he returned, as she ran down the steps to throw her arms round him.

"I will tell you about it," Sir Richard had said, and his voice did not sound like his own.

It was almost impossible to comprehend that the turn of a single card should cause such a disaster.

By every law of averages Sir Richard should have won the last game, in which he had risked everything, including the Castle and the Estate, against the Earl's stake of fifty thousand pounds.

But as her father had said, the Earl of Stanbrook was invincible. Appropriately enough, he had turned up the ace of spades and Sir Richard was finished.

His wife and family heard the news in silence, too stunned even to ask questions.

The next day, on their father's orders, they started to move out of the Castle and into the smallest house on the Estate, Dovecot House, which had been empty for some years.

It was in its own way an exquisite example of Elizabethan architecture, with diamond-paned windows, small rooms with beamed ceilings, and a garden that was redolent with roses and honeysuckle, lavender and syringa.

But it was no consolation for the home that had been so much a part of them that they felt crippled without it.

They missed the round Tower overlooking the sea, the huge Baronial Banqueting-Hall which had been added later, and the fine State-Rooms which their grandfather had redecorated in the most extravagant manner.

They felt lost without the portraits on the walls of the early Rockbournes, most of whom had been soldiers and extremely handsome and whose descendents all had the same distinguishing characteristics.

Anthony looked exactly like the Rockbourne who had been painted by Van Dyck, and it was easy to see Marista's large luminous eyes and straight little aristocratic nose in the portraits of her grandparents and great-grandparents.

Letty was so lovely that Sir Joshua Reynolds, who had painted her mother, would have been the only artist who could capture the beauty that reminded anybody who saw her of the flowers that grew in the Castle gardens, especially the magnolias that bloomed throughout the summer.

At first even Lady Rockbourne could not believe that they had to leave everything behind them.

"Surely the paintings would bring us a fortune," she suggested.

"I lost the Castle, its contents, and the land on which it stands," her husband replied with an edge to his voice that sounded like a cry of pain.

Because in everything he was honourable, he allowed them to take with them to Dovecot House only their own personal belongings and nothing that he had inherited.

Only after the tragedy of their father's death, which had shattered them to the point where they hated the Earl of Stanbrook so violently that they longed to hurt him as he had hurt them, did Anthony creep back to bring out from the Castle several things that he had been told to leave behind.

Marista still found it almost incredible to recall the moment when they realised they would never see their father again.

It was a very hot day. Sir Richard had come down to breakfast in the small Dining-Room of the house, which seemed like a tinder-box after the large Morning-Room at the Castle.

He had seemed quiet and morose, but as that had been his mood ever since they had moved from the Castle, nobody thought it particularly remarkable.

Only his wife noticed that he ate nothing and pushed aside the cup of coffee she had poured out for him as if it would choke him.

He had risen to his feet to say:

"It is hot! I am going for a swim."

It was something he often did in the summer, so again nobody was surprised.

"I hope you do not want me to come with you, Papa," Anthony had remarked. "I want to ride over to see General Grange to see if he has improved on the offer he made for the Phaeton. I do not think it is enough."

"I agree with you," Sir Richard said. "Get as much as you can, and give the money to your mother."

"I intend to drive a hard bargain," Anthony replied firmly.

His father did not seem to hear him. Instead he went round the table to bend down and kiss his wife.

"Take care of yourself, my darling," he said, "and do not do too much."

She turned to him for a moment to say:

"And do not stay too long in the water. I have no wish for you to catch a chill."

He had kissed her again without saying anything and then had left the room.

When he was gone, Lady Rockbourne had said almost as if she spoke to herself:

"Poor Papa! He is so miserable and unhappy over what has occurred, and I do not know how to comfort him."

"What can you do, Mama," Marista had asked, "except try to make him realise that wherever we are, as long as we are together we can be happy?"

"I am not really happy," Letty objected, who was only fifteen at the time. "I hate the pokey little room in which I have to sleep. I want my lovely big room at the Castle, and when I am grown up, how can you ever have a Ball for me without a Ball-Room, Mama?"

Her mother had sighed and Marista had seen the pain in her eyes.

She turned and put her arm round her mother's neck to say:

"Darling Mama, I am sure things will come right. Perhaps Papa's luck will change, and we will be able to buy back the Castle and live there again."

Her mother kissed her cheek.

"I hope . . . so too . . . darling," she had answered.

Her voice had broken on the words and she had hurried from the room so that her daughters would not see her tears.

There was every reason for them.

As the hours went by and Sir Richard did not return, Marista had gone down to the beach to look for him.

She went down the twisting path with steps cut into the cliff which led to some rocks, but there was no sign of him.

Just a little way to her right, the sea swept into the caves which lay beneath the Castle, which she knew at times were used by smugglers.

Occasionally the local fishermen crossed the Channel to bring back a small amount of contraband goods which were not enough to command the attention of the overworked Revenue Officers.

They were busily employed in trying to prevent the large and dangerous gangs farther along the coast from carrying into France good English gold, which Napoleon needed desperately.

Now as the tide was coming in, the waves had already filled the bottoms of the caves and would soon rise very much higher.

Her father was very unlikely to be there, and Marista looked in the other direction and thought she saw something lying on the beach.

It took her a little time to reach it, and she found, as she had suspected, that it was her father's robe made of towelling, which he habitually wore when he walked from the house down to the sea.

She picked it up and cradled it in her arms, feeling that she must hold on to it, and it would somehow prevent her from thinking of something so terrifying that she was desperately afraid of what her mind suggested to her.

"No, no! Please, God, not that!" she prayed, and looking out over the water she searched for a long time for a sight of her father's head swimming back towards her.

But there was only the emerald green-blue of the sea moving restlessly and ceaselessly, unheeding that in it a man's life could end as swiftly as a thought.

Only after she had stood on the shore for nearly two hours did Marista carry her father's robe back to the house.

Her mother met her as she entered the garden, and she did not have to ask. She knew what had happened from the expression on her daughter's face and the robe which she carried in her arms.

For a long moment Lady Rockbourne stood quite still.

Then without a word she turned back and went into the house, and Marista knew that she had lost not only her father but also her mother.

Her father's body was washed ashore on another part of the coast two weeks later.

He was brought home and buried in the Churchyard of the small Norman Church which had been built at the same time as the Castle Tower.

People from the County, the villagers, and everybody on the Estate had come to the Funeral and sent flowers.

However, there was nothing from the Earl of Stanbrook, and Marista, looking at her mother's white face and eyes dark with pain, thought she hated him more than ever.

It was he who had been responsible for her father's death, and when her mother died five months later, having no wish to live in a world that did not hold the man she loved, Marista had blamed the Earl again.

It was not just that he had beaten their father at cards. That was a game of chance, but Marista thought the way he had behaved in taking over the Castle and the Estate was unnecessarily callous and heartless.

Almost before they had moved their possessions into Dovecot House, the Earl's representative, a middle-aged Attorney, arrived.

He appointed two caretakers to live in the Castle and be responsible for it.

He then ordered the shutters to be fastened over every window and the doors to be locked, and without speaking to anybody on the Estate or to Sir Richard or Lady Rockbourne, he had left.

The only other people who were to be employed, they learnt later, were two gardeners and two Keepers.

Otherwise, the grooms and the labourers were all given two weeks' wages without any expressions of gratitude for what they had done in the past or any interest in what might happen to them in the future.

"How can anybody be so heartless?" Letty had asked plaintively.

Marista remembered that her father had replied:

"He seems to have no feeling. He is indeed a man without a heart, and I know now that everything that has been said about him is true."

That did not make it any easier to bear the humiliation their father felt, and the fact that he had not been consulted and had been ignored from the moment he handed over the deeds was no longer of any importance to him.

But Marista, who adored her father, understood perhaps better than Anthony and Letty how he could no longer live in a world where he had become a nonentity, exiled from the Castle that was part of his blood.

She often lay awake at night wondering what her

father's thoughts had been as he swam farther and farther out to sea, knowing that when he drew tired there would be no chance of his being able to return.

There were treacherous currents in the English Channel once the swimmer was beyond the protection of the cliffs, and she prayed that her father had died quickly and at the end had not struggled against his own decision to end his life.

Only when her mother had joined him in the grave on which they put flowers every week did she realise that she had to take her mother's place and keep the family together.

Anthony was already restless, wanting money so that he could go to London and hating being confined in a tiny house, and, although he was the sixth Baronet, feeling of no importance because he was penniless.

"It is fortunate that since the Earl never comes here you can still ride over the land," Marista said comfortingly.

"What on?" Anthony had asked sharply.

"We have two horses left."

"Only because they are so decrepit nobody wanted to buy them!" her brother answered.

"Oh, dearest, I am sorry," Marista had exclaimed hopelessly.

He put his arm round her and held her close against him.

"I am afraid that I sound like a bear with a sore head," he apologised, "and I know it is as difficult for you as it is for me. You ought to be dancing every night at Balls in London, instead of which you are stuck here in this dead-and-alive hole with no money and nobody at all interested in any of us, now that we no longer own the Castle."

It was depressing to find how the friends who had surrounded her father and mother melted away, Marista thought.

She tried to dismiss the thought but could not help knowing that this was not only because they were poor but because as a family they were all too attractive, too good-looking.

No ambitious mother would want her daughter to be enamoured of Anthony, who at twenty-one was so handsome and so fascinating that on seeing him any girl's heart would beat faster.

Because of his father's death he had to leave Oxford, and there was nothing for him to do but walk about aimlessly on the land that had once been his, and ride the only two horses they had left because they were unsaleable.

Marista was well aware that because she and Letty were so pretty, they outshone and spoilt the chances of any friends of their own age.

They were therefore firmly left off every invitation list where the hostess's daughter might find them in competition in what was undoubtedly a social Marriage Market.

As it happened, Marista was not worried about herself, and her thoughts were always about Anthony and Letty.

Because she adored her brother she pressed his coats and polished his Hessian boots until they shone far more brightly, she was quite convinced, than those of any Buck or Beau in St. James's.

But that did not give him money to go to London, which was what he really wanted to do.

Once or twice since their mother had died he had in some mysterious way suddenly been able to "indulge himself," as he called it, for a week or so.

"How can you afford it?" Marista had enquired.

There had been a pause before he answered, and he did not look at her when he did so.

"I manage, and somebody is helping me."

"Who is that?" Marista questioned, but he seemed not to hear her.

But going to London and enjoying himself only made his return more depressing, and she thought it was very brave and commendable of him to work at training the horses of a neighbouring farmer.

In fact, some of his service was so menial that he did not like to speak of it, but it provided the only income they had on which to keep themselves alive.

Every day Marista wondered if they would ever be able to keep their heads above water and not be swamped by debts which accumulated however hard she tried to manage. Now this bombshell had arrived.

"Two hundred fifty pounds!" she cried. "Oh, Letty, Letty, what am I to do?"

"There is only one thing you can do."

"What is that?" Marista enquired without much hope in her voice.

"You must go and see the Earl and tell him we cannot pay."

"See the . . . Earl?" Marista exclaimed in horror.

"There is no use talking to anybody else about it," Letty said. "It is the Earl who has demanded rent for the house when we thought it was ours, and you will just have to make him understand."

"I . . . cannot do . . . that! Of course . . . I cannot!" Marista exclaimed.

"Then the alternative," Letty said, "is that his Agent, or whoever that horrible person is who has written the letter, will turn us out of the house and into the street!"

Marista looked at her sister with startled eyes.

"Can he do that?"

"Of course he can! That is what Agents do, and I do not suppose he would even bother to tell the Earl about it."

"I cannot do it . . . Letty! I cannot . . . bear to speak to . . . him!"

"Then I will!"

"No . . . of course not!"

As she spoke, Marista remembered all the stories she had heard about the Earl, of the ladies who had loved him to distraction, of the women he had under his protection, and she knew that one thing she must never allow was that he should see Letty.

She was well aware how lovely her sister was, and she would have known it even if the people in the village were not constantly telling her so.

When they went to Church every Sunday it seemed impossible for the members of the choir to look anywhere else except at Letty's golden pink-and-white beauty.

Because she was unaware of it herself and had received no compliments since she had grown up, Letty was completely unselfconscious, and Marista was sure she had no idea that men stared at her as if they could hardly believe she was real.

Now she turned from her contemplation of the garden and said in a different way from the way in which she had spoken before:

"No, I see it is I who must talk to him, and perhaps he will be more sympathetic than if Anthony did so."

"I am quite certain if you let Anthony see him it will end in an argument. You know how bitter he is at the way we have to live, knowing also that the Earl is responsible for Papa's death."

'I am bitter too,' Marista thought.

However, she knew she would be too tactful to say so, especially if she had to plead for the Earl's mercy.

The idea of approaching him filled her with horror, and she felt that the humiliation it involved was almost too great to bear.

However, she knew how her mother would have behaved in the same position, and there was really nothing she could do but throw herself on the mercy of the man she loathed.

She looked at Letty, and said in a voice that trembled:

"Supposing when I go to the . . . Castle . . . he refuses to . . . see me?"

# Chapter Two

Driving towards the Castle, Marista felt more and more nervous.

Her first idea had been that she should walk from their own small garden through the Park and into the garden of the Castle.

It was only a short distance that way, but if she went round by the drive then it would be nearly half-an-hour's walk.

It was Letty, however, who said:

"You cannot walk. It would look as if you were a beggar from the village. I will come with you and we will drive."

"In what?" Marista asked.

The Phaeton, the Chaise, and even the brake in which their guests' servants and luggage used to be brought to the Castle had all been sold to meet the debts that were still outstanding after her father's death.

Everything that was of any value had gone, including her mother's jewellery and furs.

Although even this had not raised enough to pay the creditors in full, they had accepted that something was better than nothing and ceased to trouble them.

As she stared at her sister in surprise, Marista then remembered there was the old Governess's cart, in which they had driven as children.

It had become very dilapidated over the years and was worth so little that the men who had bought her father's carriages had merely looked at it with disdain and left it where it was.

Marista and Letty had gone to the stables and cleaned and polished it until it still looked old but fairly respectable.

Then they put between the shafts the better of the horses, the only one that it was really possible to ride for any distance.

Only by cosseting them and feeding them well, which they could not really afford, had the two broken-down animals, which their father out of kindness had saved from the knackers' yard, been kept serviceable.

When Sir Richard had drowned himself, Anthony, because he could not bear to be in the house, had ridden them round the Estate until they almost buckled at the knees.

Now as he was breaking in horses for Farmer Dawson he was too tired in the evenings to wish to ride, and the horses had become fat and lazy.

She and Letty usually found it easier to walk to the village when they required anything than to have to groom and saddle the horses in the stables.

As it happened, Marista liked walking and would often climb down the steps and walk along the beach, sometimes thinking of her father but more often telling herself imaginative tales.

In these everything was happy again, and they were helped to find a mythical treasure by mermaids from the sea, or nymphs from the woods, or angels from Heaven.

Because she had a vivid imagination Marista thought herself into her stories until she was a part of them and sometimes it was difficult to know where fantasy ended and reality began.

Now, driving towards the Castle with Letty beside

her, she faced the hard reality of having to go down on her knees to a man she hated and beg him for mercy.

"If he refuses, what can we do?" she asked.

She was so frightened of the answer that she looked despairingly at Letty, who, reading her thoughts, said:

"I am sure it will not be as bad as you fear."

"What can be worse than having to . . . meet the Earl?"

"How do you know?" Letty asked. "He might not be as bad as we think he is."

"I talked to Papa about him one evening before he died," Marista said in a low voice. "It was after dinner when you and Mama had left the room. Because he had had a lot of claret to drink, he was not as reserved and silent as he had been since it all happened."

"What did you ask him?" Letty asked curiously.

"I said: 'When you were playing that terrible game, Papa, in which the Earl of Stanbrook won everything that belonged to us, did he goad you into playing for such high stakes?'

"Papa thought for a moment. Then he said:

" 'I do not think that is the right word, and I am trying to be truthful, Marista. It was not what he said, but what he was. Do you understand? He was so self-assured, so confident, so supremely aware that he would win that it was a challenge which neither I nor any other . . . sportsman could have . . . resisted.' "

Marista's voice died away on a little sob, and Letty said:

"Do not upset yourself, dearest. I cannot help thinking that if you arrive in tears the Earl will not like it. Men always hate weeping women. Just plead with him for all our sakes and try to make him feel a little guilty because of what he has done to us."

Marista was about to reply that it was quite impossible for her to do such a thing, when the Castle came in sight, and as always ever since they had been obliged to leave it, she felt its very beauty was like a stab in her heart.

It was so romantic and so much an intrinsic part of her that she felt as if her name were written on the stones.

Slowly, because Rufus was never in a hurry, the horse plodded between the ancient oaks, over the bridge which spanned the lake, and up the short incline which led to the gravelled courtyard in front of the steps which led to the iron-studded front door.

Almost without meaning to, Marista took in the fact that the glass in every window shone brilliantly, the gravel in front of the steps had been raked, there was not a weed to be seen, and the steps themselves had been scrubbed until they were as clean as the cravats she washed and ironed for Anthony.

Then as if she forced herself to be practical she said to Letty:

"Take the reins, Letty, and stay here until I come out, and do not speak to anybody. Do you understand? I will not have you mixed up in this mess or have anything to do with His Lordship or his friends."

Letty did not reply, and too late Marista thought it was a mistake to have brought her.

Even in the plain cotton gown that Hannah had made for her and with a cheap straw bonnet on her fair hair, she looked so ridiculously lovely that she might have stepped down from the clouds or come from the flowers in the garden.

Letty took the reins in her small hands, which unconventionally were not gloved, and Marista, opening the door at the back of the Governess's cart, climbed down to the ground.

She took a deep breath and, holding her chin high, walked up the steps to the front door.

By the time she reached it somebody inside must have heard the wheels on the gravel, for it was opened.

There were four footmen inside the big Hall, and a Butler who Marista thought looked like an Archbishop.

The latter stepped forward to say in a respectful voice:

"Good-morning, Madam!"

"I wish to see the Earl of Stanbrook."

Even to herself her voice sounded quite calm, and the Butler replied:

"I will inform His Lordship of your arrival, Madam. May I have your name?"

"Miss Marista Rockbourne!"

As she spoke Marista felt as if her ancestors in the paintings on the stairs stared at her reproachfully.

And yet at the same time it was somehow comforting that they were there, and that the Earl had neither thrown them away nor consigned them to the attics.

The ancient flags were also hanging on either side of the big stone mantelpiece, and because they had been won by Rockbournes in battle, she felt as if they gave her courage and told her not to be afraid.

The Butler led the way across the Hall and opened the door of the small Drawing-Room.

It was the room in which her mother had always sat, because the windows opened onto the rose-garden.

Because it was so familiar and so fulled with memories, for a moment it swam in front of Marista's eyes and she moved blindly towards the sofa without really seeing it.

Only when the Butler had shut the door behind him was she able to look round and realise how much the room had been altered.

The curtains had been changed and so had the carpet. There was also a great deal of French furniture which Marista thought was doubtless very valuable.

There were new paintings on the walls, and she recognised a Fragonard and a Boucher, but the portrait of her mother painted by Sir Joshua Reynolds still held pride of place over the mantelpiece.

She looked up at it, and because it resembled her mother so closely she said almost as if she were there:

"Help me, Mama . . . if he will not do what we ask, we shall have . . . nowhere to go and it is . . . frightening to think of . . . it."

Because her appeal was also a prayer, Marista strained every nerve in her body with the intensity of her feelings.

Then she knew it must be her imagination, but her mother seemed to smile at her and the expression in her grey eyes was comforting.

Because she was concentrating on the portrait, Marista did not hear the door open, and only when she was suddenly aware that there was somebody advancing towards her did she start and turn her head.

For a moment she was motionless, for the Earl was all she had expected him to be and a great deal more besides.

He was tall and broad-shouldered, but it was not his height that was so impressive, but the fact that he was in himself so overwhelming, and the moment she saw him she knew why her father had called him a challenge.

He was not only supremely sure of himself, but he also looked, Marista thought, as if everything and everybody else were beneath him and he condescended to them from a great height.

She was so bemused by the Earl's appearance that only when he said in a dry cynical voice: "You wanted to see me, I believe?" did she rise quickly to her feet and drop him a curtsey.

"I am grateful to . . . Your Lordship for . . . doing so," she managed to reply.

She spoke in a soft, hesitating murmur because she was overwhelmed by the Earl, and he said:

"I imagine you must be the daughter or some relation of Sir Richard Rockbourne."

"I am his elder daughter, My Lord."

"And he sent you to see me?"

For a moment Marista stared at him, finding it difficult to understand the question. Then she answered:

"My . . . father is . . . dead."

The Earl raised his eye-brows.

"I am sorry. I was not informed. I had not heard that he had died."

Marista did not speak, and perhaps it was the expression in her eyes and the sudden pallor of her skin that made him ask:

"What happened? He seemed perfectly well when I last saw him."

It was difficult to speak, but Marista forced the words to her lips.

"M-my father went swimming in the sea soon after we had been obliged to leave the Castle, and he never . . . came back."

The Earl stared at her as if he could hardly believe what she was saying. Then he said in a somewhat gentler tone than he had used before:

"Suppose you sit down, Miss Rockbourne, and tell me why you are here."

Marista sat on the edge of the sofa, her hands in her lap.

She hoped the Earl would sit too, but instead he stood with his back to the mantelpiece and she was forced to look up at him. At the same time her mother's portrait was behind him, and she felt that in some way it sustained her.

The Earl was staring at her and she was not surprised when he said:

"I presume the painting behind me is a portrait of your mother?"

"Yes . . . it is . . . My Lord."

"You are very like her. Is she with you?"

"No . . . My Lord . . . she too is . . . dead."

"But you are still living near here?"

Marista's eyes were wide with surprise as she exclaimed:

"You . . . you do not . . . know?"

Even as she spoke, she was aware that Letty had been right when she said that if his Agent turned them out doubtless the Earl would not even be told about it.

With what seemed a superhuman effort she said:

"I . . . I came to see you, My Lord, because this morning at breakfast-time we received a very . . . upsetting letter . . . addressed to my . . . mother."

The Earl did not speak and Marista went on:

"It was from your Agent and he . . . ordered us to pay . . . rent for . . . the house in which we . . . live."

"Which house is that?" the Earl asked.

"It is called Dovecot House, My Lord, and I thought, and I am sure my mother thought so too, that when we moved from the Castle . . . at least it was ours to . . . live in without . . . payment."

The Earl said in a dry voice:

"I am sure my Agent would find that a very optimistic assumption."

Because of the way he spoke, Marista felt her fear of him replaced by the hatred that had been in her breast ever since her father had died.

She suddenly realised how unimportant they were to a man who had everything, and the fact that he had neglected the Castle for over two years was somehow insulting, and not made any less so by the fact that he now expected them to pay for the years when he had ignored them.

Her chin went up as she said:

"Since you won the Castle and the Estate from my father, My Lord, and we were told to move out . . . immediately, we have had no . . . communication of any sort from either . . . you or those who . . . represent you."

"I had in fact forgotten that this Castle existed until a month or so ago," the Earl said.

The way he spoke and the indifference in his voice was to Marista like a slap in the face.

She had no idea how her grey eyes that were so like her mother's suddenly sparkled with fire as she said:

"We have not forgotten, My Lord. We are doing our best to exist, or rather keep . . . alive, and although you have . . . killed my father and my mother, there are still . . . three of the family left."

The Earl stared at Marista as if he could not believe anyone so small and insignificant would speak to him in such a manner.

Then as if Marista realised she had gone too far and the Earl would doubtless tell her to leave without saying any more, she added quickly:

"Forgive me . . . I should not have . . . spoken like that. I came here to . . . beg for mercy . . . not to . . . offend Your Lordship . . . in any way."

"Are you really accusing me of causing the deaths of your mother and father?" the Earl asked.

Marista made a helpless little gesture with her hands.

"I do not suggest you . . . meant to kill Papa intentionally . . . but he went to London to gamble because we were in desperate straits, and he said that you . . . yourself constituted a . . . challenge that he could not . . . ignore."

The Earl moved to sit down in an armchair facing the sofa before he asked:

"What did your father mean by that?"

"He said . . ." Marista began, then she stopped. "No . . . Your Lordship will . . . think me . . . rude. Can we please go back to . . . where we . . . started?"

"I am interested," the Earl said, "and if I do constitute a challenge in myself, it is something nobody has ever told me before."

Marista looked up at her mother's portrait. Then she said:

"What Papa was referring to was not your expertise or your sportsmanship, but the fact that you are so . . . assured . . . confident and quite . . . certain that you will be the . . . victor."

"I suppose that is a compliment."

"I am not flattering Your Lordship," Marista said quickly, "but now that I have seen you I can . . . understand exactly what . . . Papa meant."

"You mean that I am a challenge to you?"

"I do not . . . want you to . . . be," she replied. "I want you to be . . . generous when I tell you that we . . . cannot pay the rent and if you . . . turn us out of the house, my brother, my sister, Letty, and I will . . . starve."

"You have a brother?"

"Yes."

"How old is he?"

"Anthony is twenty-one."

"And what is he doing?"

"He had to leave Oxford after Papa lost everything to you, and he is now training horses for a local farmer and earning fifteen shillings a week. That is literally all we have to live on, except for about fifty pounds a year we receive from a legacy left to Mama by one of her relations."

"You mean you have . . . nothing else?" the Earl asked.

"We manage," Marista said quickly. "We keep hens, we buy fish, which is quite cheap, and we grow our own vegetables."

The Earl looked at her as if he could hardly believe what he was telling him was the truth, and she said:

"You do understand, My Lord, that as that is all we have, we cannot possibly pay the two hundred fifty pounds in back rent which your Agent has demanded. And incidentally, I do not think it fair to ask suddenly for such a large amount, whether it is from us or from the farmers, who are finding it very hard to make ends meet."

"Surely, Miss Rockbourne, you are not troubling your head about them at the moment?" the Earl remarked.

Because she thought he was sneering at her, Marista said again a little aggressively:

"They were . . . our people, My Lord, before you took them . . . from us, and my father was always deeply . . . concerned about them and helped them in every . . . way he could."

As her voice died away she felt as if she could read the Earl's thoughts, and she was sure he was thinking that if her father had been really concerned with the people who relied on him, including his family, he would not have gambled in such a foolish manner.

"I see you are prepared to take me to task," the Earl said after a moment, "but as I have already told you, Miss Rockbourne, I leave to my Agents such matters as collecting rents and dealing with tenants. I have a number of Estates, and to concern myself with each one of them would take up all my time."

There was silence. Then Marista said in a voice that trembled:

"Are you . . . telling me . . . My Lord . . . that we have to . . . obey your Agent?"

Before the Earl could reply, the door opened and a young man dressed in the height of fashion came hurrying into the room.

"I say, Uncle Nevlin," he said to the Earl, "there is the most beautiful girl I have ever seen in my life outside the front door! Can I invite her in? She is so lovely that I cannot believe she is real!"

Before the Earl could reply, Marista jumped to her feet.

"That is my sister, My Lord," she said. "She accompanied me here, and we must leave . . . immediately!"

The Earl did not move.

"Why?"

"Because, My Lord, I have nothing more to say. I must go home and try to think of some plan by which, unlike . . . my father and mother, we can . . . survive."

Although she tried to speak proudly and defiantly, her voice broke on the last word and she felt not only as if God had failed her but also her mother looking down from the portrait over the mantelpiece.

The young man came farther into the room.

"So that is your sister," he said to Marista. "Now I can see there is a likeness between you, and you are very beautiful too. How can there be two such lovely women here at the end of nowhere?"

The way he spoke was so ingenuous that Marista was able to say in a calm tone of voice:

"Thank you, Sir, but I must . . . go at once to my . . . sister."

"I say—you cannot leave like that!" the young man cried.

He looked at the Earl.

"Please, Uncle Nevlin, will you not introduce me?"

The Earl rose slowly to his feet.

"But of course, Peregrine," he said. "Miss Marista Rockbourne, may I present Lord Lampton, my nephew, who, as you have already realised, is extremely impulsive and considers himself a connoisseur of beauty."

There was no doubt that the Earl was being sarcastic, but Marista ignored him and curtseyed to Lord Lampton, who made her an extremely elegant bow.

"Now that we are introduced, may I bring your sister into the house?" he asked. "I am sure you would both like some refreshment."

"Thank you," Marista replied, "but we have to return home."

"Before we have finished our conversation, Miss Rockbourne?" the Earl enquired.

Marista was hating him so violently that she dared not look at him. Instead, she said in a low voice:

"I think . . . My Lord, there is . . . nothing more to . . . say."

"On the contrary, I have a great deal to say," the Earl contradicted, "and I think it would be to your advantage to listen to me."

Marista was suddenly still.

She felt as if he had thrust her into the very depths of despair, in which the darkness was so impenetrable that she could think of no way out.

Now suddenly there was a faintly glimmering light of hope that made her raise her eyes to his face.

He looked at her for a long moment. Then he said to his nephew:

"Of course, Peregrine, bring in the young lady you have met outside. After your romantic eulogy, I am of course eager to meet her."

It was then that Marista remembered the Earl's reputation, and below her breath she said involuntarily:

"No . . . no!"

She thought she had not spoken loud enough for him to hear her, but his ears must have been sharper than she had anticipated, for as Lord Lampton hurried delightedly from the room, the Earl said:

"From your tone of voice and the expression in your eyes, Miss Rockbourne, I deduce that you have no wish for your sister to meet me."

There was nothing Marista could say. She merely lowered her eyes, and her eye-lashes were long and dark against her pale skin.

Desperately she tried to think of a reply, and as the Earl did not speak she managed to say:

"Letty has . . . always been . . . brought up in the . . . country, My Lord. She is very . . . unsophisticated and . . . inexperienced."

"And do you mean to keep her for the rest of her life consorting with cabbages and country yokels who will not appreciate her beauty if it is anything like your mother's?"

It was extremely difficult to answer this question, but Marista was sure he expected her to, and after a pause she said:

"Now that Mama is dead, I am hoping that Letty will meet some . . . young people of her own age . . . but as there are no . . . neighbours who . . . entertain us . . . that is not going to be . . . very easy."

"But there must be some young people round here, even though Peregrine seems to think it is the end of the world," the Earl contended.

"We had many friends when Papa and Mama were . . . alive," Marista replied defensively.

She felt it was somehow an insult to her father and mother that the Earl should think they too were cabbages or country yokels.

"What is happening now?" the Earl enquired.

Marista hesitated, and he went on:

"Shall I guess? Two beautiful young women do not fit very easily into families where they are likely to provide too much competition for the hostess's daughters."

Marista thought he was far more perceptive than

she had expected. At the same time, because she felt
he challenged her, she could not help saying:

"It is worse, My Lord, when the girls in question
are . . . penniless and have not the . . . background
they had when . . . their father and mother were . . .
alive."

"You mean of course the Castle."

"Yes . . . the Castle."

Her voice trembled as she spoke of it, knowing
how much it had meant to all of them, and how once it
had stood for home, security, and happiness.

She was aware that the Earl was staring at her, and
she thought his eyes, which were dark and penetrating,
and seemed to look deep into her heart, were as detest-
able as he was himself.

She knew that her father had been right in calling
him a challenge: he was so strong, so pulsatingly alive,
that he made her acutely aware of him as a man, and
she shrank from such awareness almost as if he were
touching her.

There were voices outside, and a second later Letty
came into the room.

She was smiling at something Lord Lampton had
said to her, and she looked so exquisitely beautiful that
although Marista was apprehensive about her meeting
the Earl, she knew he could not but acknowledge that
she was lovely, and she was sure that Letty could hold
her own with any Beauty who was acclaimed in London.

Quite unselfconscious and not in the least shy,
Letty walked towards the Earl and dropped him a
curtsey.

She looked up at him as she did so and said as she
rose:

"You look exactly like I thought you would, My
Lord, and I have been longing to meet you."

"Why?" the Earl enquired.

He had a way of asking questions in monosyllables that seemed to Marista frightening, but Letty merely smiled.

"If you lived here you would know that was a foolish question," she replied. "Nothing ever happens from day to day, from month to month. Then suddenly vans started arriving at the Castle and it was naturally very exciting."

"I think your sister feels rather differently about it."

The way the Earl spoke made Letty look at Marista, then back at him.

"You have not been cruel to Marista?" she asked. "I have been sitting outside praying that you would be kind and understanding."

There was a faint smile on the Earl's lips as he answered:

"Are your prayers, Miss Letty, usually answered?"

"I would say as a rule they have an odds-on chance," Letty replied. "But in this case it is very, very important that they should win."

The Earl gave a little laugh and Lord Lampton, as if he resented that Letty was not talking to him, said:

"Where do you come from? And how can you appear in a place like this unless you have arisen from the sea?"

"I come from here," Letty said, "this Castle, and your uncle, like a wicked Ogre, has turned us out!"

She spoke impulsively, and Marista drew in her breath.

"Please . . . Letty . . . please!" she said quickly.

Letty looked up at the Earl and said:

"I was very rude. Please forgive me. But we have thought about you like that for nearly three years! We are, however, quite prepared for you to change into a benevolent Genie, or even a kindly Monarch, if you will let us stay at Dovecot House without paying any rent."

40

"Rent? Do you mean to say you have to pay rent for living on my uncle's Estate?" Lord Lampton asked. "He ought to pay you to do so. Why, if people in London saw you they would all be coming down here begging for his houses and paying astronomical sums for them!"

"That is a wonderful idea!" Letty laughed. "Then Anthony and I would not long to go to London, for London would come to us."

"So that is what you want!" the Earl interposed. "And what about your sister?"

"Marista is so good that she does not complain, and she never cries as I do because she has not had a Ball given for her in the Castle. Mama always promised we should both have when we came out."

"What Uncle Nevlin ought to do is give one for you," Lord Lampton said.

Letty's eyes sparkled.

"That would be a splendid idea!"

"I should enjoy it too!" Lord Lampton added.

The Earl walked to the mantelpiece to pull the bell.

"I think you are moving too fast, Peregrine," he said, "and I suggest we have some refreshment while the two Miss Rockbournes tell us a little more about themselves."

As he finished speaking the door opened and the Butler stood there awaiting instructions.

"A bottle of champagne," the Earl ordered, "and also some lemonade in case the young ladies prefer it."

"Very good, M'Lord."

"I think," Marista said nervously, "we should leave as I was . . . intending to . . . do."

"I have already told you, we have not yet finished our conversation, Miss Rockbourne," the Earl replied, "and I am quite certain that my nephew has a great deal to say to your sister."

41

"I have indeed!" Peregrine agreed. "What about my showing you the Castle, Miss Letty?"

Letty laughed.

"I think it would be much more appropriate if I showed it to you, seeing that I know every stone, every corner, and everything else about it."

"Then I should be delighted for you to guide me from the battlements to the dungeons!"

"I think," Letty replied demurely, "it would be unconventional for us to wander away on our own, and Marista would not approve."

For a moment Peregrine Lampton looked sulky. Then he said:

"Well, at least we might look at the view."

"But of course," Letty agreed. "It would be quite proper to, so long as we see it either from inside or just outside this room."

As she spoke she walked with a grace that was indescribable towards the window, and Marista stared after her with an open mouth.

She was astounded to hear Letty talking like that and behaving in such a sensible and collected manner that she could hardly believe what was happening.

The Earl looked amused as he watched the expression on her face. Then he said:

"I thought you told me that your sister was unsophisticated? She certainly knows how to manage an impetuous young man."

"I cannot . . . think . . . how!" Marista said almost to herself.

"I believe all women have a natural instinct for self-preservation," the Earl said. "You appear to consider yourself responsible for your sister, but I am sure you need have few fears on her account. She can undoubtedly look after herself."

"I hope that is true," Marista replied, "but she is so . . . beautiful!"

She spoke the thought in her mind spontaneously, forgetting to whom she was speaking, and she started when the Earl asked:

"Have you never looked in the mirror?"

"Of course!" Marista replied.

"Then you must realise that two beautiful girls are more sensational than one, and I really think, Miss Rockbourne, you should do something about it."

"I . . . I do not . . . understand what . . . you are . . . saying, My Lord."

"As my nephew's idea of bringing London here is somewhat impractical," the Earl said, "perhaps it would be easier for you and your sister to go to London."

Marista laughed and for a moment it swept away the worry from her eyes.

"It would be just as practical, My Lord, to suggest that we fly to the moon or dive down to the bottom of the sea. I suppose because you are so rich you are still finding it difficult to realise that it is hard enough to find money for food, let alone to travel, to wear beautiful clothes, or to entertain!"

"I am not as obtuse as you think," the Earl said. "At the same time, I think you will agree, Miss Rockbourne, that beauty, like talent, should not be hidden under a bushel."

"What I am asking at the moment, My Lord," Marista replied, "is that we can stay at Dovecot House and not have to starve."

"But from what you have told me, you are not far from that unenviable state," the Earl remarked.

Because Marista thought he was mocking her, her hatred for him, which for the moment had been forgotten through surprise at Letty's behaviour, came flooding back.

"I would like . . . My Lord," she said in what she hoped was a practical, businesslike voice, "to know . . . exactly where we . . . stand."

"It is somewhat difficult to answer your question," the Earl replied, "until I have seen Dovecot House, estimated its worth, and of course got to know the occupants a little better than I do at the moment."

"I cannot think why we should be of any interest to you, My Lord," Marista replied coldly. "You live in one world, but we live in another."

"At the moment we are living near to each other in what I might almost agree with Peregrine is the end of the world. A few steps farther, and we should be in the sea!"

Because she thought he was disparaging the Castle and its location, Marista asked:

"Why have we come here? Why . . . why should you want to open the Castle and confront us with all these . . . problems?"

She gave a little sigh before she went on:

"I came to see you the moment I received the letter, and I am wondering if perhaps everybody else on the Estate and in the village, which you own too, received the same sort of communication from your Agent! All those people will be anxious . . . in fact . . . terrified for their . . . futures."

"Do you think that is what they will be?"

"Of course . . . and . . . they will be hating you."

"As you do!" the Earl said quietly.

The way he spoke brought the colour into her cheeks.

Because she was looking at him when she spoke, she would not allow herself to look away, but faced him defiantly.

"You hate me!" he repeated. "I saw it in your eyes when you first saw me, and I suppose it is understandable."

"I know it is . . . wrong to hate . . . anybody," Marista murmured. "At the same . . . time . . ."

She stopped to feel for words, and the Earl finished:

"I am the exception."

There was a note of cynicism in his voice, and again Marista thought that he was laughing at her.

"I do not . . . want to hate you," she said, "and I do realise that you did not mean to . . . kill Papa. It was a game of chance, and it was very . . . very foolish of him to . . . think he could . . . settle his debts that way. But . . ."

Again she paused, and the Earl said:

"Go on!"

Marista decided to tell him the truth, and she said:

"I think the way we were turned out of the Castle was unnecessarily cruel," she said quietly, "and it was intolerable that you did not discuss with Papa what was best for the Estate and those who have served our family for generations, which hurt him very much."

"I can see that now," the Earl agreed.

However, Marista thought he spoke not in a conciliatory way but condescendingly.

"Papa was very proud," she went on, "and you not only ruined him but hurt his pride. You made him feel insignificant and inferior, which was . . . unnecessary and . . . unfair from one . . . sportsman to . . . another."

The Earl was silent and Marista continued:

"I should not say all these things to you, and I am sure it is only making you . . . incensed with me. But you did ask me, and I am afraid that, being one of the cabbages and yokels you sneer at, I say what is in my mind without any social grace."

"You are being honest, Miss Rockbourne," the Earl replied, "and you may not believe it, but I like honesty and frankness, which is something I do not often hear."

"I do not . . . usually say such . . . things," Marista said in a different tone, "and I came here meaning to . . . hide my feelings and . . . to plead with you to

45

help us in a way you would have found . . . hard to . . . refuse."

"Why did your intentions and plans go wrong?"

"Perhaps because our . . . conversation has been . . . somewhat unusual," Marista answered, "and Lord Lampton and Letty . . . interrupted me when I was . . . leaving."

"Not having obtained your objective?"

"You said you . . . intended to . . . leave everything to your . . . Agent."

"I said that is what I usually do on my Estates. But as I have just said, I would like to see your house, and, having met both you and your sister, I think it would be a good idea if I met your brother as well."

For a moment Marista's eyes lit up. Then she looked away to say quickly:

"I think that would be a . . . mistake."

"Why?"

Here was another of the Earl's monosyllabic questions, and after a moment she replied:

"I think it would be a mistake because if Anthony sees . . . you and meets your nephew, he will be . . . more restless and miserable than he is at the moment."

"You mean he will be envious?"

"Of course he will! He was so happy at Oxford, and he loves going to London. There is nothing for him to do here, no friends of his own age, no dances, no Theatres. Nothing but work and the fifteen shillings a week, which barely keeps us in food."

There was silence before the Earl said:

"I can see your brother means a great deal to you."

"I love him as I love my sister," Marista said, "but it is not easy to keep them happy and prevent them from thinking all the time of the . . . past, which I know is a . . . mistake."

"What do you think about?" the Earl enquired.

"I find it best to live from . . . day to day," Marista said in a small voice. "The past is . . . gone, and the future . . . frightens me. Perhaps God will . . . answer my prayers, but He is taking . . . rather a long time . . . about it."

Again she spoke without thinking, and she thought the Earl might laugh at her. But instead he said:

"I would still like to meet your brother. I am sure it would please my nephew as well as myself if you would dine with me this evening."

"No . . . no . . . we cannot do . . . that!" Marista cried.

But as at that very moment two footmen came into the room bringing the refreshments, she thought the Earl had not heard her.

\*     \*     \*

Driving home after Lord Lampton had assisted them most attentively into the Governess's cart and the Earl had stood on the steps to watch them go, Marista felt as if her head were in a whirl.

She tried to say that they could not dine at the Castle, but Letty accepted the invitation with such enthusiasm and so much excitement that it was somehow impossible to make herself heard.

"I will send a carriage for you at seven-thirty," the Earl said. "I keep London times and not country ones."

"We always dined at eight o'clock," Letty said, "because Papa liked to be out while it was daylight, and he too preferred London customs to country ones."

"I stand corrected," the Earl said with a laugh.

"Now you are trying to snub me," Letty protested. "I know you are thinking that we do not know how to behave, but we are not as ignorant as you think."

"You are putting words into my mouth that I had never thought of," the Earl argued.

"As it is a long time before dinner," Lord Lampton interposed, "could I not call on you this afternoon?"

Before Marista could reply, Letty said:

"Of course you cannot! Marista and I have to spend the afternoon concocting something to wear. We have not been invited out for simply years, but naturally we do not wish to look like the Beggar Maid to King Cophetua!"

"Is that who you think I am?" Lord Lampton asked, laughing.

"No, of course not," Letty replied. "I have told you already that I have changed your uncle from being the wicked Ogre into the King of the Castle!"

"I am extremely gratified at the transformation," the Earl remarked.

There was a twinkle in his eyes as he spoke, and Marista thought that he was fascinated by Letty.

'He will not of course wish to marry her,' she thought. 'He will go back to London and leave Letty with a broken heart, and it will be as bad as when he killed . . . Mama.'

Because she was so anxious, she said to Letty as Rufus moved and they were crawling slowly up the incline of the drive:

"What did you think of the Earl?"

"He is overwhelming," Letty replied, "and although Papa was more handsome and in a way more dashing than he is, I can understand that he could not win against him."

"Why should you think that?" Marista asked, intrigued.

"Because I am quite certain that to oppose the Earl would be like throwing one's self against the Castle Tower and attempting to knock it down."

"I know what you mean, but I was really asking what you thought of him as a man."

"Rather old and very difficult!" Letty replied.

Because the way she said it sounded rather funny,

both girls laughed. Then there was silence until Letty said:

"You know, Marista, when I have read plays, I have always thought it would be very difficult to flirt and be witty and amusing as in a Restoration Comedy, but when I was talking to Lord Lampton it seemed to come quite naturally."

"I have certainly never heard you talk before as you were talking to the Earl," Marista remarked.

"I have never had the opportunity," Letty said. "But the plays I have read have made me long to have a chance of practising repartee, or what one writer called 'duelling with words.'"

"I thought it very clever of you, dearest," Marista admitted. "At the same time, it sounded a little rude and precocious."

Letty shrugged her shoulders.

"What does it matter?" she asked. "You know as well as I do that we are swept away with excitement at meeting the Earl and his friends. But the moment he begins to be bored he will go back to London, and we will never see him again."

Marista looked at her sister in astonishment.

"Why should you think that?"

"It is what Lord Lampton told me. He says his uncle decides to go somewhere, then almost before he arrives he starts to yawn and moves on again."

She bent forward to lay her hand affectionately on her sister's arm.

"But do not worry, dearest. I am going to enjoy myself and not take seriously anything flattering that is said to me, nor count on the Earl and his nephew on being here more than a few days."

She gave a little sigh before she said:

"I shall miss them when they are gone, but I am sensible enough to know it will not last."

"You are very, very wise," Marista agreed.

"And what about you? Did you get him to agree that we could stay without paying any rent?"

"I do not know," Marista answered. "For one moment I thought it was hopeless and got up to leave. Then Lord Lampton came in and said he had seen you, and afterwards the Earl insisted that he should visit the house to meet us all. So I think, although I hardly dare say it to myself, that he might agree, if we are very, very tactful and do not upset him."

Letty gave a little cry.

"Oh, Marista, you are clever! But I thought you were being rather difficult with him in arguing when you should have been saying yes, yes, yes!"

Marista drove on for quite a little while before she said:

"I have been wondering if the reason why the Earl gets bored is because he has so many people saying 'yes, yes, yes' in his life."

"It might be," Letty agreed. "At the same time, Mama always said that men like to feel they are right and hate women to argue with them."

"Papa said once," Marista answered, "that he liked a good chase and it was a great mistake for either a fox or a woman to be caught too easily!"

"That is exactly the sort of remark Papa would make!" Letty replied, and they both laughed.

Only as they reached home and took Rufus back to the paddock did Letty say:

"Now hurry up, Marista. You know as well as I do that I was right when I said we have to find something to wear for this evening. But Heaven knows we have not much choice."

"He will have to take us as we are," Marista replied. "As you pointed out, whatever we look like, the Earl is bound to be bored, and we might as well just enjoy ourselves and forget what kind of impression we are making on him."

"That is what I call good thinking," Letty said. "At the same time, because he is so supercilious, I want to surprise him, and that, Marista, is exactly what we will do."

# Chapter Three

M arista looked at herself in the mirror and said: "I think we look somewhat . . . theatrical."

"Nonsense!" Letty replied. "And if we do, it will at least make people notice us, and do not forget, all the other ladies will be glittering with jewels."

"The other ladies?" Marista questioned.

"The house-party," Letty explained. "Lord Lampton told me the guests were arriving this afternoon."

"I had no idea," Marista murmured.

A sudden thought struck her and she looked at her sister in consternation.

She remembered her father speaking of the rowdy and often exotic parties which noblemen gave in London, and in her own mind she had always connected them with the orgies of the Romans.

Letty knew what she was thinking and laughed.

"Do not be so ridiculous, Marista!" she said. "The Earl may be raffish and wicked from your point of view, but his sister is staying in the Castle, and he is not likely to do anything outrageous while she is there."

"His sister!"

"I thought he would have told you. The reason he came to the Castle was that his sister, Lady Lampton, has been ill and the Doctor said she was to go to the sea

52

to convalesce. It was then that the Earl condescended to remember that he owned our Castle."

Marista gave a little sigh.

It would have been so much better, she thought, if he had gone on forgetting.

Yet, because Letty was so enthusiastic about the evening, she could not help joining in the fun of finding an evening-gown amongst those that had been put away in a wardrobe after her mother died and had not been looked at since.

They needed pressing, and the sisters spent the afternoon with Hannah in the kitchen, heating flat irons at the fire.

Their faces were flushed by the time they had finished, but it was satisfying to know that even Hannah approved of the appearance of the gowns, and it was fortunate that there was very little alteration needed except on Letty's, who was smaller than her mother.

Because it was only at the very last moment that their father's debts became so menacing that he could not keep them hidden any longer, Lady Rockbourne had always been elegantly gowned, although she did not patronise the fashionable over-expensive dressmakers.

The fashions had not changed very greatly in the last few years, owing to the war.

Letty told Marista that gowns, instead of being straight and unadorned, were now embroidered round the hems and bodices, while the plain ribbons which had crossed over the breasts at the beginning of the century were now discarded in favour of flowers, frills, and lace.

"How do you know such things?" Marista asked.

"When we lived at the Castle," Letty replied, "Mama always took *The Ladies' Journal*. Then when we moved here we could not afford such luxuries, but Hannah has often borrowed one from the Vicar's wife."

"Why should Hannah want *The Ladies' Journal*?" Marista asked in surprise.

"For the crochet patterns," Letty replied. "But I looked at the fashions, the gowns, and the hair."

It was therefore Letty who arranged first her own hair, then Marista's, and when they put on their mother's pretty but sparsely adorned gowns, Marista saw that Letty had decorated them in an original manner.

At first Marista could not think what her sister could be collecting in the garden, until she came back with a large basket filled with flowers and leaves.

"I really do not think we will want all those to make a small wreath," she said.

Letty did not answer, but she started to work on Marista.

Her gown was very soft blue, which had been a perfect frame for Lady Rockbourne's beauty as it was for hers.

Letty decorated the hem of the gown with tiny moss roses that were just coming into bloom and put with them their small, pale green leaves, stitching and pinning them into the light gauze of the gown in an artistic manner.

She also added roses in the low décolletage and arranged a little cluster on each of the small sleeves.

When Marista looked in the mirror, she could hardly believe that anything could be so pretty, although in her opinion it was too spectacular.

"You look lovely, dearest!" Letty said. "Now take off your gown very, very carefully, so as not to crush the roses, and help me with mine."

Letty's gown was white, which Marista thought suitable for her age, but she was determined that it should be striking. She had therefore picked a large number of white camelias that were growing on one side of the house.

They might on their own have been somewhat

insipid, but three rows of them and their dark glossy green leaves made the gown look as if it came from Paris, which of course was impossible during wartime.

"You are sure it is not too much?" Marista asked nervously.

Letty shook her head.

"I am going to wear three camelias and some leaves on the top of my head," she said. "I think you should have just two little roses above your left ear, and nothing else."

"I think I ought to have something that will make me look older, and perhaps more . . . dignified," Marista said tentatively. "After all, I am your Chaperone."

Letty laughed.

"I will chaperone myself. All you have to do, dearest, is to look lovely, just as if you have stepped out of a painting by Sir Joshua Reynolds, and the Earl can look up at Mama in the Drawing-Room and compare her with you."

Marista did not tell her sister that the Earl had already said that she looked like her mother.

Instead she lifted her chin a little higher than usual and said:

"I am sure that whatever we do the Earl will think we look like two country yokels, so, as you have said, we might as well enjoy ourselves, except that I shall be worrying all the time whether he is going to allow us to stay here or turn us out."

She sounded so frightened that Letty said:

"Forget it and enjoy yourself as I am going to do. We may never again be asked to dine with anybody so important, and whatever the Earl may think of us, Lord Lampton is very effusive in his admiration."

"You must not believe everything he said," Marista said quickly.

"I may not believe but I want to listen," Letty

55

replied. "The compliments I receive in this part of the world are few and far between."

When the Earl's carriage arrived for them, on Letty's instructions Marista sat down gingerly on the edge of the seat so as not to bruise the flowers round her gown.

Letty gave Anthony, who had joined them at the last moment, having been fiddling for hours with his cravat, strict instructions not to let his legs touch their gowns.

He was, Marista thought, as excited as Letty at the idea of dining at the Castle, and he did not seem to feel, as she did, that it would be upsetting to see somebody else in their father's place.

Hannah had pressed his evening-coat, which had belonged to his father, and she and Letty had ironed every white muslin cravat he possessed so that if he spoilt one in trying to tie it, he could pick another.

He looked smart and very handsome, and she wondered if there would be any women there who would find him alluring, and perhaps for one evening at any rate help him to forget the menial tasks he was forced to do at the farm.

Letty would not let Marista put on a wrap in case it crushed the roses on her sleeves.

"It is a good thing it is a warm night," Marista said, "otherwise we should arrive coughing and with blue noses, which would be very unbecoming."

"We will survive," Letty replied, "and if we cannot be the smartest women present, we might as well be original in some way or another."

Marista looked at her sister with worried eyes.

"Please, Letty, do not do anything of which Mama would not approve. The Earl may think we are country bumpkins, but we know how to behave like ladies."

"It would be much more fun and it would teach him a lesson," Letty said, "if we turned up with straw in our hair, looking like looney milk-maids, and talked in a heavy Sussex dialect."

"In which case he would certainly turn us out of Dovecot House," Marista said.

"I can always offer you a haystack at the farm," Anthony remarked.

They all laughed at the idea. At the same time, when the carriage came to a standstill outside the front door of the Castle, Marista suddenly had an impulse to pull the roses off her gown and try to appear as inconspicuous as possible.

She was sure the Earl would think they were deliberately trying to attract attention, and once again she was afraid he might break Letty's heart.

Too late she wished she had been strong enough to refuse his invitation to dinner.

When they entered the Hall and saw a number of footmen in attendance and heard the noise of voices in the Salon which her father and mother had only used when they were entertaining, she felt her heart beating feverishly in her breast, and her lips were dry.

But Letty's eyes were sparkling, and as they went up the staircase, which had been embellished with a new carpet, Marista was aware that her sister was not in the least shy but was already enjoying the excitement of her first large party.

The Butler announced them.

"Miss Marista, Miss Lettice, and Sir Anthony Rockbourne, M'Lord!"

The candles in the huge crystal chandeliers in the Salon had been lit, and it seemed to Marista as if the Earl came towards them in a blaze of light, and her imagination told her that if he had not sold his soul to the Devil, he was perhaps the Devil himself.

'I hate him! I hate him!' she thought, and tried not to look at him as she rose from her curtsey.

"I must introduce you to my friends," the Earl

said, and drew Marista towards what seemed to her an overwhelming crowd of fashionably dressed people standing at the end of the Salon.

As Letty had predicted, the ladies were glittering with jewels and were not only exceedingly beautiful but, Marista thought, haughty and hostile, while the men, equally resplendent, seemed to fawn over her and Letty.

At that moment she would have given anything in the world to be able to run away, back to the safety of Dovecot House.

Somebody, and she supposed it was the Earl, placed a glass of champagne in her hand, and she held on to it tightly, as if it were a lifeline that would save her from drowning.

She heard a dozen names as she was introduced, but she could not remember any of them, and their faces, with the exception of the Earl's and Lord Lampton's, were just blurs.

Then a lady who she realised was the Earl's sister, because she seemed in her own way as impressive as he was, said to her:

"I understand you owned this Castle before it became my brother's property. It is exceedingly attractive. I had no idea any building could be so near to the sea."

"It was first built in Norman times," Marista replied. "My father told us that there were always sentinels on guard at the top of the Tower, watching for enemies whether they came by sea or by land."

"How thrilling!" Lady Lampton remarked, and Marista felt she was sincerely interested in what she had just been told.

Before she could say any more, the Earl was at her side, and because instantly she was acutely aware of him, her voice seemed to die away in her throat.

"If you are talking about the Castle," he said, "I

am hoping you will tell me about the secret passages which I understand exist in many parts of the building."

Marista drew herself up.

"If there are any," she replied, "and I am not admitting that there are, they are known only to the head of the Rockbourne family, and are passed on by him to his eldest son before he dies."

"I see I shall have to talk to your brother."

"I am quite certain that Anthony will not tell you what should be known only to a member of the family," Marista said.

As she spoke she saw that the Earl's eyes sparkled, and she thought that once again they were battling with each other, and on this point, as in everything else, he was determined to get his own way.

"I think, although I may be mistaken," he said, "that you know this momentous secret, and I cannot believe you would wish to leave me, as the new owner of the Castle, in ignorance, so that when I die the secret would be lost forever."

"I have not agreed that there is a secret, My Lord," Marista protested.

"If you will not tell me that," the Earl continued, "what about the smugglers who I understand still use the caves beneath us?"

Marista was very still.

She was well aware that when the fishermen had bad hauls at sea, they slipped across the Channel to bring back a cargo, the sale of which tided them over until they could fill their nets again.

She also suspected that many of the villagers, who were always impoverished but could ply an oar, used to go with them.

She not only shut her eyes, as her father had done, to these activities, but was determined for very personal reasons not to ask too many questions.

Quickly she said in a voice that she tried to make as light as Letty's:

"I cannot think who has been telling you such nonsensical tales, My Lord. Smugglers are not to be found on this part of the coast, but on the Romney Marsh, where I hear their gangs are very dangerous and terrorise the local population."

The Earl smiled somewhat cynically.

"I am well aware, Miss Rockbourne, of what happens on the Romney Marsh, but smuggling all along the South Coast has become a national activity, and what could be more convenient than the caves beneath the Castle?"

Before she could reply, Anthony came to her side.

"Several gentlemen have asked to be introduced to you," he began.

Then as he just caught the Earl's last few words, he asked:

"Are you talking about the caves?"

"His Lordship has been told a lot of nonsense about their being used by smugglers."

As Marista spoke she looked directly at her brother, and she saw by the expression which came into his eyes that what she had suspected was true.

However, he turned to the Earl to say:

"You cannot believe all you hear in this part of the world, My Lord. They are always trying to frighten newcomers with stories of Highwaymen and smugglers, footpads and robbers."

"I am particularly interested in smugglers," the Earl answered quietly, "and I have in fact been asked by Viscount Melville, the First Lord of the Admiralty, to watch out for them while I am here."

Marista knew that Anthony was tense as the Earl went on:

"I expect you already know that the Revenue Cutters are overworked and find it impossible to prevent gold from being carried across the Channel to Napoleon, who is vitally in need of it to keep the war going."

The Earl paused for a moment, and it seemed to Marista that he looked penetratingly at Anthony before he finished:

"That is why the Navy is patrolling the Channel by day and by night to prevent the smugglers from reaching the coast of France."

"I can tell you a great deal more than that!" interposed a gentleman who had joined them.

"And what is that, Randolph?" the Earl asked, then said: "Forgive me, I must first introduce you. Miss Marista, may I present Lord Randolph Aldington, who is attached to the Admiralty."

Lord Randolph bowed as Marista curtseyed, and she thought that the dark-haired, somewhat ugly man facing her looked somehow sinister.

"I am delighted to meet you, Miss Marista," Lord Randolph said, "and as I have already met your sister, I am ready to believe that both of you have been smuggled in, not from France but from Venus."

To Marista he sounded like a character in one of the Restoration Plays which Letty enjoyed reading, and she thought she must remember what he had said when the evening was over.

But the Earl was back again on the subject of smuggling.

"What can you tell us, Randolph," he asked, "that we do not already know about smugglers?"

"I expect you are aware, Nevlin," Lord Randolph replied, "that Napoleon looks on the English smugglers as friends and has allowed them to build their boats in the harbour at Calais."

"It seems incredible!" the Earl exclaimed. "Although the First Lord told me that Napoleon himself had said there were over five hundred English smugglers in Dunkirk alone."

"If the war is ever going to end, we have to stop this smuggling," Lord Randolph answered, "and this is a perfect place, Nevlin, for you to watch out for these men, who are traitors as well as criminals, since every guinea they take across the Channel prolongs the hostilities."

The Earl laughed a little drily.

"You are very eloquent, Randolph," he said. "I see I will have to enlist the good services of the local inhabitants, who surely know far more about smuggling than I do."

"I can assure you, My Lord," Marista said sharply, "that we know very little about such activities, and you will find that we and the rest of the country yokels you despise are loyal subjects of King George."

"Of course we are," Anthony agreed, "and although smuggling may have existed in the past, there is no need for you, My Lord, to stay awake at night watching for boats entering the caves beneath the Castle."

"It is something I have no intention of doing," the Earl answered. "At the same time, I shall certainly offer any assistance I can to the Royal Navy and the over-strained Revenue Service."

Marista felt as if there was a warning note in his voice, and she was glad when the Butler's announcement of dinner put an end to the talk about smuggling.

When they sat down in the great Baronial Dining-Room at a table lit by golden chandeliers and decorated with a wealth of exquisitely chased gold ornaments, Marista felt she had stepped back into the past.

She remembered how as a little girl she had watched her father and mother entertaining through the carved panelling of the Minstrels' Gallery.

Now the Earl sat in her father's high-backed chair which was ornamented with the coat-of-arms of the Rockbournes, and her ancestors looked down from the huge paintings on the panelled walls with what she hoped was a condescension and a superciliousness equal to the Earl's.

She had a middle-aged Peer on one side of her, who was concentrating on his food, and Lord Randolph Aldington on the other.

He was immediately deep in conversation with the lady on his left, and Marista was free to look across the table at Letty, who was obviously enjoying herself with Lord Lampton on one side and on the other a talkative young man of about the same age.

She was looking so lovely with the camelias on her fair hair that Marista, glancing round the table, thought it was not surprising that the other lady guests were watching her with a somewhat jaundiced eye.

But there were one or two exceptions.

The two ladies who sat on either side of the Earl had eyes only for him. One was a Marchioness, although Marista had no idea of her name. The other was unknown to her but equally beautiful.

She admired the perfection of their features, but even with her unsophisticated eye she could not help knowing it was a beauty that was as brilliant and also as hard as the jewels they wore.

They were vying with each other to hold the Earl's attention, and she thought it seemed characteristic that while they pouted their red lips provocatively and their eyes offered an undeniable invitation to flirt, if that was the right word, the Earl looked bored and cynical.

'He will certainly not stay here long,' Marista thought optimistically.

From her point of view, the sooner he left, the better, because then not only Letty but Anthony would be safe from him.

She glanced down the table at her brother and saw that he too was enjoying himself, with a very pretty brunette who wore a wedding-ring but did not seem much older than he was.

They were laughing and talking, and although she could not hear what they were saying, she knew from the expression in his eyes that Anthony was finding her very attractive.

Marista gave a little sigh, thinking that although this might be amusing for an evening, he would find it harder than ever to return to the farm and the breaking in of horses tomorrow morning.

"You are very quiet, Miss Rockbourne," the Peer said to her unexpectedly, having finished the plate of food in front of him.

"I was thinking, My Lord," Marista replied, "that it is a long time since I have seen so many people in this room or heard it filled with the sound of voices and laughter."

"I understand from our host that the Castle previously belonged to your father."

"Yes."

"I remember him. A good-looking fellow, and your brother is like him."

"Yes, they are alike," Marista agreed.

The Peer looked across the table at Letty as he said:

"In fact, you are quite an astoundingly handsome family, and you are completely wasted down here. I cannot imagine that Stanbrook will find it amusing for long."

"That is what I thought," Marista agreed.

"Oh, you did, did you? Well, let me give you a tip, young lady. Do not waste your wiles on him. There are too many women trying to catch him and failing."

Marista gave a little laugh.

"I assure you, My Lord, it is the last thing I would try to do."

She spoke with such a note of sincerity in her voice that the Peer looked at her in surprise.

"You are very positive. Do not tell me that Stanbrook

does not appeal to you! I have never yet met a woman who was not after him."

"Then you have met one now, My Lord, and if you wish to know the truth, I hate the Earl!"

"Hate him? What do you mean—hate him?"

Marista realised that she had been indiscreet, and she said quickly:

"That is something I should not have said, so please forget it. But although it was my father's . . . fault that he lost the Castle in a . . . game of cards, I cannot help feeling that the Earl is an . . . interloper and the Castle is still . . . ours."

The Peer turned half-round in his chair to look at her.

"You interest me," he said, "and if you are not pursuing our irresistible host, with whom are you in love?"

Marista laughed again.

"With no-one, My Lord, I assure you. His Lordship has already informed me that there is nothing in this place but cabbages, yokels, and smugglers! None of whom, you will agree, would make particularly desirable husbands."

As she spoke she thought she was talking almost as Letty had, and she too was playing her part in a play and finding that her lines came naturally to her.

The Peer put back his head and laughed.

"What you have told me is a very sad story," he said, "and we must see what can be done to bring more attractive men to this part of the world. Shall I start by saying that I hope you will allow me to call on you tomorrow?"

He took Marista by surprise, and she said without thinking:

"Oh, no . . . please do not do . . . that. You . . . would find it . . . I am sure . . . very . . . boring."

"I am not so easily bored," the Peer replied, "and never with anybody as lovely as you."

Because she had assumed he was far too old to be interested in her, Marista looked at him wide-eyed, and as she did so she was aware that from the end of the table the Earl was watching her.

She suddenly thought that he might think both her and Letty very fast and immodest in the way they were behaving.

Although Letty had said his opinion did not matter, she thought that since they were asking a favour of him, it was important that he should not think of them in a derogatory way.

"I am afraid, My Lord," she said, "that my sister and I are very busy in our small house, and also, as my mother is dead, we have no Chaperone. It is therefore impossible for us to . . . entertain gentlemen like . . . yourself."

The Peer smiled.

"I understand exactly what you are saying to me, but having met you I assure you I have no intention of losing you, and I am certain our host will make it easy for us to keep in touch."

Marista suddenly felt afraid.

She did not know why, but she had no wish for the Earl to think she was deliberately trying to entice his friends to Dovecot House or to seek compliments she had never received before.

But there was no stopping the Peer.

"How could I have imagined," he was saying, "when I came here this afternoon at Stanbrook's invitation, expecting to spend several rather dull days in the country away from London, that I would find anyone so exquisitely beautiful and alluring as you?"

"You are very kind," Marista said, "but I would rather we talked about . . . something . . . else. What are your . . . interests . . . My Lord?"

"Beautiful women!" the Peer replied. "And as you are more beautiful than anybody I have seen for a very long time, I need not tell you that I am enjoying myself."

It was more than she was doing, Marista thought by the end of dinner.

She was not only a little frightened by the Peer's insistence, but also embarrassed by the way he spoke to her, the manner in which he looked at her, and the feeling that in some way he was encroaching on her.

He ate a great deal and drank a good deal more, but she knew from the expression in his eyes and the note in his voice that his behaviour could not be attributed to anything but the fact that she attracted him and he had every intention of telling her so.

She turned to talk to Lord Randolph in the way her mother had taught her was correct, but she found that he was deeply involved with the lady on his other side, and after a few perfunctory remarks he turned away.

The Peer saw her discomfiture and laughed.

"You will have to talk to me, pretty lady, whether you want to or not," he said. "I assure you that the situation is exactly as I wish it to be. It is not only what you say that I find so enchanting, but the movement of your lips."

He looked at her mouth as he spoke, and Marista knew he was enjoying the thought of kissing her. She stiffened and again was longing to escape from the Castle and be back in the safety of her small, low-ceilinged bedroom.

As the ladies left the room after dinner, Letty slipped her arm through hers to say:

"I have never had such a wonderful time! Oh, Marista, I am so thrilled to be here. Please, please do not try to leave too early."

As that was exactly what Marista wished to do, she

did not reply, but she thought once again that the whole thing was a mistake and it would have been better if it had not happened.

In the Salon, those ladies who spoke to them were sweetly spiteful.

"How amusing of you to wear real flowers, Miss Rockbourne," one of them said to Letty. "Do you also have a few bees or other insects hidden in your gown?"

"I am hoping," Letty replied, "that the wasps and snakes will keep away."

The lady could not think of a cutting reply, so she merely walked away. Letty smiled at Marista and whispered:

"We are a success!"

However, it was a relief when after the gentlemen came into the Salon the Earl came to where Marista was sitting to say in a proprietory manner:

"I do not expect you wish to play cards, so I hope you will answer some questions about the Castle."

Marista realised that this was his way of ordering her not to involve herself with anybody else.

She saw with relief that the Peer who had sat next to her at dinner and whose name she still did not know was already at one of the card-tables which had been erected in the Salon, and the Earl was settling his guests down to play *écarté* or *faro*.

Marista had a sudden fear that Anthony might be tempted to join the card-players and would be too proud to say he could not afford it.

Then to her relief she saw him walk through the door which led into an Ante-Room with the lady he had sat next to at dinner.

She supposed he was going to show her the Castle, and that at least would not cost anything.

Everybody seemed either to be playing at the tables or watching those who were, and it was some time before the Earl came to the sofa where she was seated alone and a little forlornly.

As it happened, she was not thinking of herself but was watching Letty, who was seated on the floor with three young men, vying with one another as to who could build the highest card-castle.

They appeared to find it very amusing and were laughing noisily, and because Letty looked so entrancingly pretty, Marista was not surprised to see a frown on the beautiful faces of the Earl's lady guests.

He sat down beside her.

"You look as if you are not enjoying yourself," he remarked accusingly.

"I am . . . sorry," Marista said quickly.

"As your host, I am sure you think it is I who should be apologising, not you."

"No . . . of course . . . not!" Marista replied. "It is . . . just . . ."

She stopped.

"Just what?"

"Just that I . . . I have never been to a party like this, and I think you were right when you insinuated that living amongst the cabbages, I would be out of my depth."

"I insinuated nothing of the sort!" the Earl answered sharply. "And I realise that Dashford frightened you at dinner."

Marista looked surprised.

"How . . . could you . . . know that?"

"Shall I say that your eyes are very expressive."

The way he spoke—drily, cynically, and somehow accusingly—did not make it sound like a compliment, and Marista blushed.

"Letty is having a . . . wonderful time," she said quickly, "and I am sure Anthony is . . . enjoying himself too."

"We were talking about you."

"I am very grateful to Your Lordship for inviting us here," Marista said, "but as you are well aware, I have so many anxieties that it is hard for me to think of anything else."

"And of course you cannot forget that I am the Ogre who has brought these tribulations upon you."

The Earl spoke mockingly, and Marista looked at him before she said:

"It was rude of Letty to say that you were an Ogre, and actually, although you are still . . . intimidating, I am not afraid of you now . . . as I was when I came . . . here this morning."

"Why?" the Earl asked in his usual abrupt manner.

"I think, although I may be wrong, that if you were going to treat us with complete indifference . . . you would not have . . . allowed us to eat your salt, and offered us your . . . hospitality."

Marista had said what was in her mind, but then was suddenly afraid that it had been a mistake to do so.

"Please . . . I am not trying to . . . force you into doing anything you do not wish to do! I am still pleading," she added, "if necessary . . . on my knees."

There was a twisted smile on the Earl's lips as he said:

"I wonder if you would really go on your knees. Looking at the faces of your rather formidable ancestors, I feel that would certainly go against the grain."

"I know it is . . . something that Papa would . . . never do," Marista said, "but if by kneeling in front of you I could . . . persuade you to be . . . kind to us, then I would forget my pride and do it . . . willingly."

The Earl looked at her penetratingly to see if she was speaking the truth. Then he said:

"Let us hope such dramatics will not be necessary. Tell me what time I may call tomorrow to see Dovecot House."

"Either before or after luncheon, My Lord."

Even as she spoke, she was aware that the Peer who had sat next to her at dinner was looking at her from across the room where he was sitting at the card-table, and she said in a low voice:

"May I ask you . . . something?"

"What is it?"

"Do not bring . . . Lord Dashford with . . . you."

"I had no intention of doing so," the Earl replied. "But there is no need for you to be frightened of him. You must learn, Marista, to take care of yourself, as your sister manages to do."

Marista noticed that he had used her Christian name, but it did not seem to matter.

"I will try," she said humbly. "But I do not find it easy, and although it may . . . seem to you very foolish . . . I am frightened of so . . . many things."

"Of myself, to begin with."

"And of Lord Dashford . . . and the ladies here, who are very, very beautiful, but who make me feel as if I had . . . crept out from . . . under a stone."

"Now you are being ridiculously mock-modest."

"What I am saying makes it sound worse than it really is," Marista admitted. "And I do try to remember that I am a Rockbourne, and that my ancestors were very brave and very, very proud."

"Then be like them!" the Earl ordered.

It flashed through Marista's mind that it was all very well for him to talk. He had everything he wanted and, as her father had said, was always successful.

It was very different from being poor, insignificant and unwanted, and frightened of the future, which was so insecure and menacing.

As if she had spoken her thoughts aloud, the Earl said suddenly:

"Good God! How can you worry when you look so beautiful? A beautiful woman, if she wishes, can have the world at her feet, or rather all the men in it."

"I am not . . . dealing with . . . men," Marista said again without thinking, "but with . . . you!"

Even as she spoke she realised the implications of her words, and the colour came into her face.

"Please," she pleaded, "I did not mean to be so . . . rude. It is just that I thought you were . . . thinking of . . . men like those . . . talking to Letty."

"I understand exactly what you meant," the Earl said, "but I still say that nobody as beautiful as you and your sister should have to worry about the present or the future, but should let it take care of itself."

"That is a gambler's outlook, My Lord, and . . . wrong."

"You have obviously not read your Bible," the Earl said unexpectedly. " *'Consider the lilies of the field how they grow, they toil not, neither do they spin, but Solomon in all his glory was not arrayed like one of these.'* "

Marista gave a little laugh. Then she said:

"You forget, My Lord, lilies have their roots firmly planted in the good soil, which feeds them and is also responsible for their leaves, which protect them."

The Earl smiled.

"Despite your fears and your humbleness, which I find somewhat irritating, you have, when you choose to use it, an unexpectedly quick brain."

"Now you are being insulting, My Lord," Marista said. "What you are saying is that it is surprising that any woman if she is pretty should also be capable of learning and of thinking and be quick-witted enough to prevent Your Lordship from yawning."

The Earl's eyes twinkled.

"Who has been talking to you?"

Marista did not wish to implicate Letty or Lord Lampton, so she said merely:

"I thought, My Lord, and you may think I am being critical, that despite the exceedingly lovely ladies sitting on each side of you at dinner, you were bored and a little cynical."

The Earl did not speak, and she went on:

"Perhaps I am being too personal, but may I point out, My Lord, that you did start it."

"Yes, I started it," the Earl admitted. "And now, Marista, because I know there are a great number of gentlemen here who wish to talk to you, I am going to change places with one of the card-players."

Marista thought she had been right in thinking that he would soon be bored with her, and as he rose she said quickly:

"Please . . . not Lord Dashford!"

"I will keep him occupied with cards until you have left," the Earl promised.

Marista found it very pleasant to talk to a soldier who had just returned from abroad and told her interesting stories of Wellington's campaign in Spain.

The Earl then introduced her to another of his guests, who was an authority on paintings. He told her, to her consternation, that several of the paintings he had seen in the passages were very valuable, although they were badly in need of restoration.

"Are you sure?" Marista asked. "I cannot believe it! If Papa had known that, he could have sold one when he was so hard up."

"Any owner of a Castle as large as this should always have its contents valued from time to time. Not only are paintings more valuable than they have ever been, owing to the Prince Regent being such an ardent collector, but also because tastes change. Two years ago, nobody was particularly interested in Dutch artists. Now their prices are rising month by month."

"If only Papa had known that!" Marista cried.

The gentleman to whom she was speaking told her where the paintings were hung, and it flashed through her mind that as the Earl had so much, perhaps he would not miss one.

When he left, they might take a painting away by entering the house through the secret passage which Anthony had used when he had collected some of the things they had left behind but which were really personal possessions.

Then she was extremely shocked at her thoughts. How could she contemplate for one moment stealing what now belonged to the Earl, even if it was a matter of no interest to him?

It was very bitter to think that he should benefit by her father's stupidity in not assessing the value of the contents of his Castle, or at least scrutinising the paintings more carefully.

Looking back, she remembered how her father had been proud of the Castle, but it had been her mother who had loved the beauty of it and had arranged the rooms to their best advantage and seen that there were always flowers to decorate them.

'Mama did not know much about paintings either,' Marista thought.

She told herself that if she was ever lucky enough to possess anything that was old and beautiful, she would make quite certain that its value was not ignored.

'How stupid! How incredibly stupid we have been!' she thought bitterly.

As she saw the Earl coming towards her with yet another gentleman, she knew she hated him more than ever, not only because he was so confident of himself but also because it seemed as if everything he touched turned to gold.

# Chapter Four

"It was a wonderful, wonderful evening!" Letty exclaimed as she came downstairs very late for breakfast.

Marista felt tired, but Letty seemed to be sparkling with vitality and excitement.

"I have never had such fun!" she went on, as Marista poured out her coffee, knowing that Hannah would be cooking her an egg in the kitchen.

"I am sure Anthony is exhausted this morning," Letty went on. "He must have felt terrible, getting up at five o'clock after he got to bed so late."

Marista had wanted to leave earlier, but she had no wish to be a spoil-sport and prevent Letty from enjoying the party.

She was also aware that having left the room with the pretty lady he had sat next to at dinner, Anthony had not reappeared, and she thought if she made any move to leave, it would be embarrassing if somebody was sent to find him.

When eventually Anthony had come back into the Drawing-Room, there was a glint in his eyes and she thought he looked more like his father than usual, because there was something raffish about him that had not been there previously.

Driving home in the Earl's comfortable carriage,

Letty had talked all the way, while Anthony had remained silent and Marista had just listened.

When they went up to bed Letty had kissed her sister and said:

"Now I understand why Papa longed to go to London and why Anthony often finds it intolerable staying here and having no money."

These were the sort of sentiments, Marista thought helplessly, that she had tried to keep Letty from feeling, knowing that lack of money imprisoned them where they were far more effectively than locks and chains.

Hannah came in with one poached egg on a plate.

"That's all there is!" she said disdainfully, putting it down in front of Letty, "and when you've finished breakfast, I'll thank you to clear the table. I'm cleaning the kitchen, and I need a bit of help."

She flounced out without waiting for a reply, and Letty laughed.

"You would think that Hannah was jealous because she was not invited to dinner with the Earl."

"I think the truth is," Marista replied, "that she is worried about you, as I am."

"Worried?" Letty questioned. "Why should you be worried about me?"

"I know it was marvellous for you last night," Marista said quietly, "but we have to face the fact that the Earl may leave at any moment, and we may not see him here for another two years or more."

"Stop croaking like an old bull-frog," Letty replied. "There is still today, and Peregrine is calling for me at noon."

Marista raised her eye-brows.

"Peregrine?"

"You cannot be so stuffy as to expect me to go on saying 'My Lord' every five minutes to him, to the Earl, and to half-a-dozen other men I met last night,"

Letty said. "It is 'Peregrine' and 'Letty,' and I feel I have known him for years."

"He will leave when his uncle does," Marista said.

Letty did not answer. She only smiled with an expression in her eyes that Marista did not like.

After a moment she said pleadingly:

"Please, Letty, be sensible. You know we cannot afford to keep up with the people we met last night, and the Earl is so unpredictable that he may decide he has had enough of the Castle today or tomorrow, and we will be left feeling flat and dismal."

Letty laughed.

"I know exactly what you are saying to me, Marista, but I promise you, I am remembering all the time that I have to hold on tight to my heart. So stop worrying!"

"I cannot help it," Marista answered.

"I thought last night when the Earl was talking to you," Letty said, "that he seemed interested in what you were saying. Do try to keep him amused so that he will stay here, and at least we can eat good food and enjoy ourselves at his expense."

"He is certainly not . . . interested in me as a . . . person."

"What do you mean by that?"

Marista did not answer, but started to clear the table for Letty, putting the cups, plates, and cutlery on a tray to carry them to the kitchen.

As she did so, she was thinking that the Earl was really interested in trying to track down the smugglers, and if he was successful, many of the people on his Estate would suffer.

She tried to close her eyes, as her father had done, to the amateurish smuggling activities that took place from time to time.

But she was aware that since the Earl, or rather his Agent, had dismissed so many employees on the Estate, those who had not been forced into serving as soldiers or sailors had been living on what they could obtain from smuggling.

The rewards were not very high because they were not in touch with the men who operated behind the big gangs at Rye or at the Romney Marsh. But there were always people with money who were prepared to pay well for a keg of good brandy or French claret, which was unobtainable in the country Inns.

Tobacco was also in demand, and Marista deliberately pretended not to notice when Anthony's clothes, left on the floor of his bedroom, were damp with sea water and smelt of tobacco.

Although she was concerned, she refused to believe her own suspicions, and because she loved her brother she never revealed what she was thinking.

If the Earl, as he had said, was helping the Admiralty and perhaps inviting the Revenue Cutters to patrol this part of the coast, then there might be a thousand new dangers she had not envisaged until now.

"I cannot . . . bear it," Marista told herself. "There is so much to worry about . . . already, and with any more we shall . . . have to . . . leave."

She knew this was just fanciful thinking, for they could not afford to leave, unless the Earl demanded his rent, in which case they could not afford to stay.

She carried the tray out of the room towards the kitchen, and Letty looked after her for a moment with a puzzled expression in her blue eyes.

She then jumped up from the table to run upstairs and decide what she should wear to go driving with Peregrine.

By the time she had put on a gown that had belonged to her mother and a bonnet that she had hastily trimmed with ribbons which belonged to another dress, there was a sound of wheels outside the front door.

When she came downstairs she found that Peregrine had arrived driving a High-Perch Phaeton, which was smarter than anything she had ever seen.

He handed the reins to the groom, stepped down, and taking her hand in his raised it to his lips.

"You are ready!" he exclaimed. "I was so afraid you might be too tired or had forgotten that you promised to come driving with me."

"I am looking forward to it," Letty replied, "because I have never had the chance of driving in anything as smart as your Phaeton."

"Is that your only reason?" Peregrine enquired, still holding her hand.

"If you are asking for compliments," Letty replied, "it is far too early in the morning for me to think of any."

"It is not too early for me," Peregrine replied. "You look very lovely, as I expect your mirror has already told you."

"Not as eloquently as I would like to hear it," Letty said, laughing.

Hearing her voice, Marista came into the Hall. Peregrine saw her before Letty did and exclaimed:

"Good-morning, Miss Marista! I expect your sister has told you that she is showing me the countryside, and we are taking a picnic luncheon with us."

"Good-morning, Lord Lampton," Marista said. "Please be very careful. I have been told that those new Phaetons with such high wheels can be very dangerous."

"Let me reassure you by saying that I am an expert driver," Peregrine replied, "and when I have something very precious beside me I am also exceedingly cautious."

"I am glad about that."

He turned eagerly to Letty.

"What I thought we would do," he said, "is to have

79

luncheon at some wayside Inn where they supply cider, if you prefer it to wine. Then there will be somebody to look after the horses and we need not take a groom with us."

Marista was just about to exclaim that she thought that would be a mistake, when Letty cried:

"That is a marvellous idea! And we can sit outside in the sunshine on the village green where the old men watch the traffic go by, if there is any, and I hope you have brought some really delicious things to eat."

"I spoke to my uncle's Chef myself," Peregrine said, "and I shall be very disappointed if you do not approve of my choice."

They looked at each other, and their eyes seemed to sparkle with an excitement that had nothing to do with the food.

Then, before Marista could protest or try to persuade them not to go alone, Peregrine had helped Letty up into the Phaeton and taken up the reins from the groom, who started to walk back to the Castle as they drove away.

"I should have stopped them," Marista rebuked herself.

She knew that she had not done so simply because it would have been embarrassing for Letty, and anyway she would have insisted on doing what Peregrine wanted to do.

Marista went back into the house feeling despondently that everything was getting out of hand, and that worst of all was the coming interview with the Earl, when he would look over the house and decide whether or not they had to pay rent for it.

'I must be very, very nice to him,' Marista thought, as she returned to arranging the flowers, which she had been doing when Lord Lampton arrived.

She knew they made the small rooms look very

much more attractive and less shabby than they did otherwise.

She was trying to decide whether if she seemed abjectly poor and pathetic the Earl would think the rent should be very much lower than his Agent had asked, or, alternatively, whether it was too humiliating that he should see her against an unattractive background.

Marista made up her mind by thinking that whatever he charged in rent they would be unable to pay it, and she therefore arranged huge bowls of lilacs in the corners of the small Sitting-Room, and elsewhere in the house vases of every other flower that was in bloom.

They were mostly simple ones which were to be found in most of the cottage gardens, and she could not help remembering that last night at the Castle she had seen hothouse flowers which she knew had been brought from London.

In the old days, carnations, orchids, oranges, and peaches had been grown in the greenhouses, which were now, after three years of neglect, sadly in need of repair.

'Perhaps the Earl will put everything back the way it was before Papa became so hard up,' Marista thought.

Then she decided that it would not be worthwhile if he was not staying long.

She had just finished arranging the last flowers in her basket when she heard somebody at the front door and thought it was the Earl.

She glanced at the clock, saw that it was noon, and was glad she had finished making the rooms look pretty.

At the same time, she had not bothered about her appearance, since she had risen several hours earlier.

She hurried to a mirror on the wall to look at herself, then put up her hands to tidy her hair.

She knew Hannah would answer the door because she had already warned her that the Earl might come before or after luncheon, and therefore she started when a voice said:

"I can see you are admiring yourself, pretty lady, and you have every reason to do so."

Marista turned round and saw with a feeling of consternation that it was not the Earl, as she had expected, but Lord Dashford.

He smiled at the surprise on her face and said:

"The front door was open, so I walked in. Let me tell you how delighted I am to see you, and that I have in fact been thinking about you all night."

A little belatedly, Marista dropped him a small curtsey.

"I was not expecting you, My Lord."

"I am aware of that," Lord Dashford said, "but I think you might have known that I would be yearning to see you again and could not wait any longer to assure myself that you are as beautiful as I remembered you to be."

As he spoke, he shut the door behind him and walked towards Marista.

As he did so, she very much disliked the expression in his eyes, and it was with the greatest difficulty that she did not run away from him.

Last night he had seemed to menace her, and now that they were alone, she was acutely conscious of danger.

"I am sure, My Lord," she said quickly, "that you would like some refreshment. I am afraid we can offer you only coffee, but I will tell my maid to make some."

As she spoke she would have passed Lord Dashford to reach the door, but as she tried to do so, he put out his hand and held on to her wrist, saying:

"I do not need coffee, but you!"

He pulled her towards him as he spoke, and Marista gave a little cry of fear. She realised he was very large and strong, and his fingers tightened round her wrist like a vice.

"Please . . . please . . . My Lord," she protested frantically.

She struggled ineffectually, and his arms were round her, holding her close against his chest.

She felt he had overpowered her and there was no escape! She could feel his lips on her cheek, hot and demanding, and she knew it was only a question of seconds before he kissed her lips.

She gave a scream of sheer fear, and as she did so the door opened and the Earl remarked drily:

"You might have waited for me, Dashford!"

Marista's heart gave a leap as she realised she was saved, and as Lord Dashford loosened his hold on her, she was free.

It was with the greatest difficulty that she repressed an impulse to run towards the Earl and throw herself against him.

Instead, she could only look at him and her eyes seemed to fill her whole face. As he came farther into the room, he seemed, because he was so tall, to fill it and make Lord Dashford shrink into insignificance.

"I had no idea you were coming here," Lord Dashford said rather disagreeably.

"I made an appointment to visit Miss Rockbourne," the Earl replied, "and I could of course have given you a lift, if you had felt inclined to tell me where you were going."

The way the Earl spoke gave the words a special significance which was not lost on his friend.

Watching the two men, Marista thought that the Earl's usual dry, cynical way of speaking held an unmistakable note of rebuke, and it was obvious that Lord Dashford too was aware of it.

There was an uncomfortable silence before he said:

"If you have business with Miss Rockbourne, Stanbrook, then I must of course bow to your prior claim and call upon her another time."

He turned to Marista and held out his hand.

"Let me say *au revoir*, pretty lady," he said, "and assure you that I deeply regret we must postpone our conversation until you are not so busy."

There was nothing Marista could do but give him her hand, and it made her shiver with revulsion when Lord Dashford touched it with his lips.

As he did so, he had his back to the Earl, and he looked into Marista's eyes with an expression which frightened her because it told her without words that although he was forced to leave now, he would inevitably return.

Then, moving jauntily so as to appear in no way disconcerted by the Earl's interruption, he walked from the room, saying as he did so:

"I will see you at luncheon, Stanbrook. I am sure the Marchioness will be waiting for you eagerly."

Marista heard his footsteps crossing the small Hall and felt as if at last she was able to breathe again. As the tension which had held her rigid was receding, she felt as if her legs could no longer support her.

"You . . . saved . . . me," she said in a voice that was almost inaudible.

"Did he frighten you?" the Earl enquired.

"It was . . . terrifying!" Marista said. "He was so . . . strong and I thought I could not . . . escape."

Her fear was very obvious, and the Earl looked at her penetratingly before he said:

"Sit down. I suppose, although it seems improbable, that this is the first time a man has tried to kiss you."

Marista sat down on a chair and felt like bursting into tears! But she knew that to lose her self-control would be very shaming, so she tried to speak lightly.

"I . . . told you," she said, "that I have met only cabbages . . . and country yokels . . . up until . . . now."

It was a brave effort, but she could not prevent her voice, like her hands, from trembling.

"Forget him!" the Earl said sharply. "I will see that he does not trouble you again."

"How can you do . . . that?" Marista asked. "I know . . . by the way he . . . looked at me that he will . . . return."

"Leave it to me," the Earl said. "Dashford is conceited and considers himself a 'lady's man,' so he will find it hard to understand that there is a woman who does not welcome his advances."

"I think he is . . . horrible!" Marista cried. "And unless I . . . lock the door, I cannot see how I can . . . prevent him from . . . coming here."

"I have told you that you are safe, and I suggest you trust me in this, Marista, if in nothing else."

Because of the firm manner in which he spoke, and because she felt he would always get his own way whatever it might be, Marista looked up at him with a new light in her eyes.

"I do trust you," she said, "and please . . . please I . . . never want to . . . see him . . . again!"

"You will not do so," the Earl said quietly. "And now, suppose we talk of something more pleasant. I find this house very attractive."

"It is . . . Elizabethan," Marista said with an effort.

"I realise that," the Earl replied, "and I think that while it may not be as impressive as the Castle, it certainly has a great deal of charm."

As he spoke he looked round the room, and almost as if she were seeing it through his eyes Marista saw how bare the walls were without the paintings that hung in the Castle.

The carpet was threadbare, and the curtains, which had been used before they came to the house, were very faded at the sides.

The furniture too had belonged to her mother and had not been inherited by her father through his ancestors.

But anything that had been valuable, like a *secretaire*, an inlaid chest-of-drawers, and some gilt-framed mirrors which had come from her mother's old home, had been sold to meet her father's debts.

As Marista's eyes followed the Earl's, she felt he was disparaging their taste without understanding that because they had been forced into giving him everything they treasured, this was all they had left, and she felt her hatred of him rising again.

However, she had underrated his perception, for as if he read her thoughts he said:

"You told me that your father was a sportsman, and I appreciate that it was very honourable that he should have been so punctilious in handing over everything he possessed without trying to keep back a great deal for himself."

What the Earl said was so unexpected that Marista felt the tears come into her eyes, and she clenched her hands together as she said:

"I wish Papa could . . . hear you say . . . that! Even Mama thought he was too honest in that he would not allow us to bring from the Castle just one or two paintings which we . . . loved, or . . . anything else that he considered . . . now belonged to you."

The Earl did not reply, and after a moment she said:

"One of your friends to whom you introduced me last night told me that several of the paintings that are hanging in the passages are very valuable."

"Are you wise to tell me that?" the Earl asked.

"When I leave for London you might have slipped into the Castle through one of your secret passages and taken them away."

Because that was what Marista had actually thought of doing and then had been ashamed of her thoughts, she started and said hastily:

"I expect your friend has told you about them."

"As it happens, he has not," the Earl replied. "So you see, Marista, you have perhaps been unnecessarily punctilious and honest."

"I think I mentioned before, My Lord," Marista said in a small voice, "that the Rockbournes have always been . . . very . . . very . . . proud."

"I am aware of that now," the Earl said, "and yet you told me that if necessary you would go down on your knees in front of me."

The way he spoke made Marista look at him uncertainly as she said almost in a whisper:

"Is that what you . . . want me to . . . do?"

For a moment the Earl's eyes seemed to hold hers captive and she could not look away. Then he said:

"I have a rather more attractive suggestion. Peregrine has taken your sister for a drive, and I too would like to drive round my new Estate, which I am sure you will say is something I should have done before. If you came with me, you would undoubtedly find it possible to point out to me not only things of interest but also those that I should repair or improve."

Marista drew in her breath.

"Do you . . . mean that?"

"My Phaeton is outside," the Earl replied, "and also a picnic luncheon. I feel you will not wish to come to the Castle and encounter Dashford again."

"No . . . indeed not!" Marista exclaimed. "And it sounds a very . . . exciting thing . . . to do!"

"And doubtless from my point of view very educational," the Earl said drily.

"I am almost ready!"

Marista jumped to her feet and gave him a little smile before she hurried from the room and ran up the stairs.

As she did so, she realised that while she had disapproved of her sister driving away for a picnic with Lord Lampton, she was only too eager to do the same herself.

"With me it is very different," she tried to convince herself as she entered her bedroom. "The Earl is taking me with him only because I pointed out to him yesterday that he should have consulted Papa about the Estate when he first won the Castle from him."

She had no time, as Letty had had, to wonder what she should wear. She had already put on her best muslin, which Hannah had made for her some months ago from a roll of material they had bought when they still lived at the Castle.

It was very plainly made and a little limp from a great number of washings, but the blue sash which encircled her waist was the colour of the sea and sky, and the blue ribbons on her bonnet, which tied under her chin, matched it.

Marista took a quick glance in the mirror and thought a little wistfully that she certainly looked a "plain Jane" compared with how she had looked last night when the moss roses, which had now faded, had decorated her evening-gown.

Then she told herself that the Earl was not likely to notice her appearance, and if he wanted elegant and fashionably dressed women, there were plenty waiting for him at the Castle.

Quickly she picked up her gloves, which Hannah had darned with tiny stitches, and taking from a drawer a silk shawl that had belonged to her mother, she hurried down the stairs.

The Earl was in the Hall, and as he watched her coming towards him it made Marista feel rather shy and self-conscious, as if she feared that she was not moving as gracefully as she should.

Then as she reached him she said:

"I must just tell Hannah I am going out. She is our old maid who has looked after us ever since we came here."

She did not wait for his reply but ran to the kitchen, where Hannah was scrubbing the top of the deal-table which stood in the centre of it.

"I am going out, Hannah, and will not be back for luncheon. Nor will Letty."

"I don't know what your mother would say!" Hannah replied gruffly. "All this gadding about will end in tears. You mark my words!"

"I hope not," Marista replied.

At the same time, as she went back to the Earl she thought that Hannah might well be right.

Whatever Letty might say, Marista was sure that when all the excitement was over she would be unhappy, and although she had not been able to talk to Anthony, she "knew in her bones," as Hannah would have said, that he would be more restless than ever.

As for herself . . .

Abruptly Marista forced her mind to concentrate on something else.

It was easy to stare in astonishment at the Earl's horses and at his Phaeton, which was in fact very much more impressive than the one Peregrine was driving.

There was a smart groom in a cockaded top-hat holding the horses' heads, and when the Earl took the reins, he jumped up in the small seat behind, and they moved off.

"Where shall we go first?" the Earl enquired.

"Do you really want to see the Estate?" Marista asked.

"I seldom say anything I do not mean," he replied in a lofty tone.

"Very well," Marista said, "but if what you see depresses you, you must not blame me."

The Earl gave a dry laugh.

"I am quite certain, however, that you blame me, Marista!"

She did not answer because she could not think of a suitable reply. She found it difficult to fight with him when it was such a joy to be driving high above the road in such a resplendent Phaeton behind two horses which she knew would have delighted her father.

She was also aware that the Earl drove superbly, and he looked so majestic that it seemed as if he came from another world altogether, which indeed he did.

'I wonder what it feels like,' Marista thought to herself, 'to know that everything you possess is better than anybody else's and to believe that you are superior to everybody you know.'

Impulsively, because it was in the forefront of her mind and she had almost forgotten that she was afraid of him, Marista asked:

"How can you be . . . bored when there is so much for you to do?"

The Earl looked at her in surprise.

"So much to do?" he questioned. "What do you mean by that?"

"Because you have everything . . . and because you are not only . . . rich and important . . . but also clever, you can, if you wish, set things to . . . rights not only on your own Estates but in other parts of the nation, and even in the . . . world."

She was following the ideas of her own mind, thinking of the Earl as a kind of Apollo with power reaching out to assist those who could not help themselves and who needed to be protected and perhaps invigorated by him.

As she finished speaking she realised that the Earl had once again turned his head to look at her as he said:

"What you have just said is something that has never been suggested to me before."

"Just as an Army needs Generals and the Government needs a Prime Minister," Marista said in her soft voice, "the ordinary people need . . . somebody to help them and to . . . understand their problems."

"Surely that is the job of the Landlords?" the Earl remarked.

"Landlords need to be led too," Marista replied, "and far too many of them, from all I have heard, spend their time in London, and the people in the country, like the Scottish Clans without their Chieftains, feel neglected and forgotten."

"You surprise me!" the Earl said again.

Because she thought the way he spoke was drier than usual and perhaps a little bored, Marista said:

"I am . . . sorry if I am being . . . tiresome. It was just an . . . idea that came into my . . . mind."

Realising that she was not playing the part the Earl expected of her, she began to point out the cottages that needed repairs and told him that pensioners were finding it very hard to live on the same amount that her father had given them, which had been continued when the Earl took over but had not been increased.

"You see," Marista said nervously, "things have grown very much more . . . expensive as the war has . . . dragged on. A shilling does not go as far as it used to . . . nor does a penny . . . for that matter."

"I think the pensioners on my other Estates receive

more than they do here," the Earl said, "and certainly I will look into it."

"If you . . . could do that it would be . . . very kind."

She thought it a mistake to over-emphasize the point, and she took the Earl first to the farm of Mr. and Mrs. Johnson.

There they heard the same dismal tale which Marista and Letty had listened to every day: that they lacked help because they could not afford to employ labourers while their sons were away at war, that all the roofs had holes in them, and that the stock could not be replaced. After they had left, the Earl said:

"I think now it is time for luncheon, and I definitely feel in need of food and drink."

Marista looked at him apprehensively.

She liked the way he had listened patiently to everything the farmer and Mrs. Johnson had told him, and while she had not heard what he said in reply, because she had gone back to the Phaeton, thinking it was tactful not to eavesdrop, she was aware that both the old farmer and his wife were beaming with smiles as they waved him good-bye.

'Perhaps I am being over-critical,' she thought to herself.

On her directions, the Earl drove to where about two miles from the Castle there was a place where she had picnicked ever since she was very small.

It was in the ruins of an old Abbey where some of the walls still stood and part of the Cloisters.

There was a well in the centre, from which the monks had drawn their water, and now covered with moss and ivy it was very picturesque.

The groom laid out their luncheon on a large slab of marble in the Cloisters, where they were protected from the wind and from anybody watching them while they ate.

The Earl took off his hat and sat down on one of the stone seats which years ago Marista's father had arranged in front of what served as a table.

"I dislike picnicking on the ground," her father had said firmly, "and as we shall doubtless come here over the years, we might as well make ourselves comfortable."

Marista told the Earl the story, and he remarked:

"I think your father was very sensible. I too dislike having to lounge about while I eat."

Marista laughed.

"It is a good thing you are not a Roman! I have always thought that lying on a couch at a feast must have made it impossible to use a knife and fork."

"I think the couches were more useful for the orgies which took place afterwards."

Marista blushed as she remembered how after what she had heard about him, she had expected that the Earl would have orgies at the Castle.

He saw the colour in her cheeks and asked:

"What do you know about orgies, Marista? I cannot imagine they are suitable reading for pure young girls."

Marista's blush deepened and the Earl went on:

"Perhaps, just as Letty thought of me as an Ogre, you have been imagining me as a debauched Roman Emperor like Nero."

Because this was so very nearly the truth, Marista could not look at him, and he asked:

"Now what can have put that idea into your head?"

"It was not . . . exactly what I was . . . thinking," Marista replied, "but there is some semblance of truth in it . . . just a very little."

"I had no idea," the Earl remarked after a pause, "that my reputation could have reached the wilds of Sussex, and of course—you."

"I am sure that Letty and I were just using our

imaginations," Marista said uncomfortably, "and because we hated you we naturally invented terrible stories about you."

"And now that you have met me, am I worse or better than you expected?" the Earl enquired.

"When you came into the room and . . . saved me from . . . Lord Dashford, I thought that you were like a 'Knight in shining armour.' "

She paused before she added a little mischievously:

"I am only a little . . . disappointed that you did not . . . slay the dragon!"

"Do not worry," the Earl replied, "I will do that later!"

They talked during luncheon, and when they finished Marista exclaimed:

"That was delicious!"

The Earl poured a little more of the champagne into her glass, then filled his own.

"You must tell my Chef so. He complained bitterly that he had not been given enough time in which to prepare the sort of meal he likes doing."

"I cannot imagine it could possibly have been better," Marista said.

Even as she spoke she realised that she had in fact eaten almost without being aware what each dish was, simply because she found it so exciting to talk to the Earl and battle with him in words.

She could not explain it to herself, but she felt, because he was confronting her and she was opposing him, that almost every word they said was a point scored, first by one, then by the other.

It was an excitement she had never known before, and she had no idea that her eyes sparkled when she thought she had confounded him, and that he waited with an interest he seldom showed in anything for her reply to some remark he had made.

Because he had taken off his hat, she had removed her bonnet. Living in such an isolated spot, she seldom wore anything on her head when she was out-of-doors.

Now the sunshine picked out the soft lights in her hair, and although it did not sparkle like Letty's, it waved softly against her oval forehead and her cheeks.

She had not tried to repeat the fashionable way in which Letty had arranged her hair last night, but had just twisted it into a chignon at the back of her head.

Because it was very simple and unsophisticated, it in fact accentuated the perfection of her features and the translucence of her skin.

The Earl was aware that she was too thin because of the frugal way she lived, so that her eyes seemed unnaturally large in her face. But when she laughed it was with the spontaneity of a child.

As he watched her, he thought she was completely natural in everything she did, and there was nothing artificial about the way she looked or what she said.

"I suppose we ought to go on with our tour of inspection," Marista said as the Earl finished his glass of champagne.

"There is no hurry."

"I have so much to show you."

"We need not do everything in one day."

"But perhaps you will go back to London and then I shall reproach myself for not having drawn your attention to something very important which needs to be done and will remain neglected entirely through my fault."

"If you are taking my sins upon your shoulders, Marista," the Earl said, "I am afraid you will find them a very heavy burden."

She thought he was insinuating that she was being presumptuous, and she looked away from him and said in a small voice:

"I do not wish to . . . impose upon you . . . and you must . . . forgive me if you are . . . finding this very . . . tedious."

"I have not said so."

"But it must be very dull for you, and Letty will be very angry if I drive you away too quickly."

"So Letty wants me to stay."

"Of course she does," Marista answered. "At the same time, I think it would be a . . . mistake, and I was going to . . . ask you something . . . if I got the chance."

"Well, you have the chance now," the Earl said, "and I am listening."

Marista found it difficult to find words. Then she said:

"I am afraid . . . desperately afraid . . . that your nephew or somebody like him staying with you at the Castle . . . will break Letty's . . . heart."

The Earl looked amused.

"Would that matter so very much?"

"Of course it would!" Marista said fiercely. "It is one thing for elegant young men like Lord Lampton to amuse themselves for a short time with a pretty, unsophisticated country bumpkin, but you know as well as I do that when you leave, your house-party goes with you, and none of you will ever think about us again."

"Do you really believe what you are saying?"

"I am talking sheer commonsense, My Lord," Marista answered. "Lord Lampton is charming and very eloquent, and Letty assures me that she does not believe what he tells her! But as they are the first compliments she has ever been paid, I know it will be very difficult for her not to take them seriously."

"Is that something you will do yourself?"

Marista thought of Lord Dashford and shuddered.

"I hope I would never be so stupid as to listen to . . . flattery and mistake it for an expression of . . . real love," she replied slowly, as if she were speaking to herself.

"And how, without experience, would you know the difference?" the Earl challenged.

"I have never been in love," Marista said, "but Papa and Mama loved each other, and when they were together it was almost as if they were surrounded by a . . . light which came from within . . . themselves. It was the love they had for each other . . . the love which made them . . . unhappy when they were not . . . together."

She paused before she added:

"When I came back from the beach after waiting for two hours for Papa to . . . return from the sea, I did not have to . . . tell Mama what had . . . happened. She knew . . . and in that moment she too . . . died."

The way Marista spoke was very moving.

There was a silence, but because she thought the Earl would consider she was being over-emotional, she surreptitiously wiped a tear from her cheek.

She jumped up from where she had been sitting and walked across to one of the ruined windows of the Abbey which overlooked the countryside.

She stood staring out at the trees beneath them and beyond to where the land ended and the sea began.

It was a very warm day and there was a mist over the horizon where sky and sea joined, and silhouetted against it were the turrets and Tower of the Castle, looking strong and impregnable.

Marista was staring at it as she felt the Earl join her, and for the first time she thought that because of his strength it was a very fitting background for him.

He saw where she was looking and said quietly as he stood beside her:

"Do you feel it is still yours?"

She did not think it strange that he should understand her feelings and her thoughts, and she replied without considering what she was saying:

"Yes . . . and wherever we may be . . . whatever happens in the future . . . it is still part of us! Yet somehow at this . . . moment it seems . . . right that . . . you should be . . . there."

# Chapter Five

Marista was only half-asleep when she heard the door of her bedroom open and thought vaguely that it must be later than it seemed.

Then somebody was beside her bed, saying in a low voice:

"Marista, wake up!"

She opened her eyes and saw in the dim light that it was Anthony.

"What is it?" she asked. "What is the matter?"

"I have something to tell you."

She pushed herself farther up against her pillows to ask:

"What is the time?"

"It is five o'clock."

She stared at him and asked:

"Why are you up so early? It is Sunday."

On Sunday, when he did not go to the farm, Anthony always slept late, sometimes, if he was tired, nearly until luncheon-time.

Then she realised that he was dressed, and he answered:

"I have not been to bed."

Marista made a movement with her lips, then as her eyes grew accustomed to the dawn light coming from between the curtains, she realised that his hair was blown over his forehead, he was wearing his very old clothes, and a handkerchief was tied round his neck.

As she looked at him she remembered that he had been missing yesterday evening, and when she had asked where he was, Hannah had said he had come in for a short while in the afternoon, then had gone out again.

When he did not appear for supper, she had said to Letty:

"Do you think Anthony is at the Castle?"

"If he is, I shall be very annoyed that the Earl did not ask us," Letty replied.

Marista did not tell her that she knew the reason they had not been asked.

When after luncheon she and the Earl drove home after she had shown him a great deal more of the Estate, he had said:

"Because I know you do not wish to meet Dashford again, I will not invite you to the Castle tomorrow. He is leaving first thing on Monday morning, so I shall expect you all to dine with me that evening."

Marista was surprised to find herself feeling happy that he would not be leaving with his guests, but she told herself that it was only because she would be able to show him more of the Estate.

As if he followed the reasoning of her mind, the Earl said in his usual dry manner:

"You must give me time, Marista, to digest all the things you have shown me so far, some of which I find extremely indigestible."

Marista had drawn in her breath.

"I am sorry if it seems dismal," she said, "but the war has upset so many people, and while the farmers in some parts of the country are, I believe, making money, the soil here is not very good!"

She paused and added:

"Also, because we are near the sea, every able-bodied man has been press-ganged into the Navy."

"Sailors are essential if we are to win the war," the Earl commented.

"I realise that, but the tenant-farmers on . . . ou your Estate . . . suffer in consequence."

She struggled over the word "your" because she had been about to say "our" and was aware that the Earl had noticed it.

However, he made no comment, and they had driven on to the next farm which Marista wished to show him.

There she was very careful to emphasise that it belonged to him and that he was responsible for what must be done if it was to prosper.

Only when they had said good-bye did she say in a small voice:

"What I have shown you may have been boring, but I can only . . . hope and . . . pray that you will . . . want to make this . . . tiny part of . . . England happy."

As she spoke she had the feeling that perhaps she had pushed him too far, but he merely replied:

"Shall I promise you that I will think seriously about it?"

He had brought her home later than she had expected, and now she thought that she should have worried when Anthony did not return from the farm at his usual time, but had come home earlier and then left again.

Now without asking she knew where he had been, and she said in a voice that trembled:

"Oh, Anthony . . . how could you do anything so dangerous . . . when . . . His Lordship is . . . here?"

"I reckoned he had not had time to get in touch with the Revenue Officers," Anthony replied simply, "and I had to have some money."

"Why did you want it so urgently?"

"Because I need new clothes and I want to go to London," Anthony replied defiantly, as if she were attacking him. "You saw how the other men looked the other night. I felt like a scarecrow beside them."

Marista gave a little cry.

"I thought you were very smart!"

"Smart!" Anthony exclaimed. "My clothes are out-of-date, and as they were not made for me in the first place, they do not even fit me properly."

Marista gave a sigh; then, feeling that there was no point in reproaching him any further, she said:

"You are back safe, and that is all that matters, but you must never·. . . never do it . . . again."

"At least this time it has been worthwhile, and that is what I want to tell you."

Marista looked puzzled.

"Why so early? You could have gone to bed and told me later."

To her surprise, Anthony looked over his shoulder as if he felt somebody might be listening to him, before he said:

"I have not come back alone."

Marista stared at him.

"What are you talking about? I do not understand."

"I have somebody with me."

"A person?"

"Yes."

"But . . . who? And . . . why?"

There was a pause, and she knew Anthony was choosing his words carefully.

The dawn light was growing stronger every moment, and now she could see that he looked very dishevelled and his hair was wet.

She put out her hand to touch his sleeve and found that it was damp.

"It has been raining," she exclaimed, "and you are soaked through! You must go and change."

"That is just what I am going to do," he replied, "but fortunately the rain was very heavy, so it was an effective way of keeping a small boat at sea hidden from prying eyes."

Marista knew this was true, but she still knew that Anthony had taken a terrible risk in crossing the Channel when Lord Randolph had said that the Navy as well as the Revenue Cutters were trying to prevent gold from reaching Napoleon.

"Do go and change," she pleaded. "You will catch a chill if you stay here."

"I am just going," Anthony said, "but listen to what I have to tell you first. I have put the passenger we brought back with us up in the attic-room, and nobody outside this house is to know that he is here."

"But, Anthony . . ." Marista began, then gave a little cry. "Supposing he is a spy? Are you sure you have not brought one of . . . Napoleon's spies . . . into . . . England?"

Her voice trembled at the very idea, and Anthony said quickly:

"No, he is not a spy. He told me all about himself—his family are English, and they were interned in France when the Armistice came to an end in 1804."

"I remember Papa saying that a great number of tourists were imprisoned then."

"There were ten thousand of them," Anthony said, "and the family of Edward Tolmarsh, for that is his name, was one of them."

"How awful! How terrible it must have been!" Marista exclaimed. "But now he has escaped."

"Yes, he has escaped."

There was silence. Then Marista asked:

"But as he is English and is now back in England, why does it have to be kept a secret?"

"He has to find his relations and does not wish to be cross-examined by the authorities about the conditions in France. He says he would rather go directly to the Foreign Office himself, and explain in his own time and in his own way."

Again there was a little silence before Anthony went on:

"He was only about fifteen when his father and mother were interned years ago because they were English, and if he now feels strange here, it is not surprising."

Anthony spoke somewhat aggressively, and because Marista was so intuitive and had always been very close to her brother, she knew that he was on edge and perhaps worried about having surreptitiously brought into the country somebody from France while they were at war.

She could not help asking:

"You are quite . . . quite . . . certain that he has told . . . you the . . . truth?"

"Of course it is the truth," Anthony replied sharply. "Why should it not be?"

"You will be in . . . terrible trouble if he is a . . . spy and is caught."

She thought Anthony's face looked drawn and white, and she said quickly:

"Go and change. You can tell me all about it later, when you have had some sleep."

"You are right," he agreed. "But I did not want you to be frightened at seeing a stranger in the house."

"We had better tell Hannah that he is a friend and had nowhere to stay for the night," Marista said practically. "She will not be pleased at having another mouth to feed."

"You need not worry about that."

Anthony put his hand into his pocket and drew out three gold coins, which he threw on the bed.

Marista looked at them in astonishment.

"Sovereigns? Did you get those in France?"

"Do you know what Edward Tolmarsh paid me for bringing him across?" Anthony enquired.

"How much?"

"One hundred pounds!"

Marista half-smiled, as if she thought he was joking. Then when she realised he was serious, she exclaimed:

"One hundred pounds? But how could he have that much money?"

"He was desperate to get away. He told me he had tried several other boats but they were too full of contraband to have room for him."

"It does not seem possible that he should pay so much!"

"I told you, he was desperate!" Anthony insisted. "I had to leave behind two kegs of brandy and two bales of tobacco, so I gave twenty-five pounds to the crew. That leaves me with seventy-five!"

"Oh, Anthony! I can hardly believe it!"

"I will give Hannah ten pounds and ten each for you and Letty, and the rest I intend to spend on myself. There will also be my share of the cargo when it is sold."

"You deserve it for the risk you ran," Marista said. "At the same time . . . this must be the . . . last time, Anthony. Please . . . promise me."

He hesitated, and she said again:

"Please, Anthony, please!"

"I will try to make it the last time," he conceded finally, "but I want to go to London, since Lady Dashford has asked me to escort her to a Ball on Wednesday night."

"Lady who?"

Marista's voice was loud with sheer surprise, and Anthony put his finger to his lips.

"Hush! You do not want to wake Letty or she will know where I have been."

"Did you say that Lady Dashford has asked you?"

"She is very pretty and very amusing."

"But . . . if she is the wife of Lord Dashford . . . she is . . . married, and I did not realise that he had a . . . wife!"

"Yes, she is married to Dashford," Anthony answered. "She is his second wife, and she told me that because he was so rich, her family pushed her into it."

"But . . . Anthony . . ." Marista began, but her brother was not listening.

"Fortunately," he went on, "he does not mind what she does as long as she does not interfere with his pursuit of other women, and so, as I find her very attractive, I want to go to London."

Marista felt as if her breath had been taken away from her and she could not think of what to say.

As she was trying to find words to expostulate, her brother smiled at her, and tiptoeing across the floor, his boots leaving a trail of wet marks on the carpet, he opened the door and was gone.

Alone, Marista could only lie back, feeling that her head was in a whirl, and it was impossible to think of a way out of the maze into which Anthony had unexpectedly plunged her.

The first thing he had done was to bring into the house a stranger who had paid an astronomical sum to come to England.

Secondly, he had told her that Lord Dashford was a married man and that he was enamoured of his wife.

"How could I ever have . . . imagined any such . . . thing?" she asked herself.

She was shocked that Lord Dashford had pursued her in such a manner when his wife was staying with him at the Castle.

Then she told herself it was just what she might have expected of the Earl's friends. At the same time, now that their immoral behaviour personally concerned both her and Anthony, she felt not only shocked but insulted.

Once again she blamed the Earl.

Why could he not have introduced Anthony to some charming young girl?

However, she knew the answer was quite simple: it was very unlikely that the Earl would have any young, unmarried women staying at the Castle, and obviously he much preferred his older friends and their wives, who were raffish like himself.

The only consolation was that if Lord Dashford was leaving on Monday, his wife would be leaving too!

Marista began to wonder frantically how she could persuade Anthony not to go to London and spend the money he had earned in such a dangerous and reprehensible manner, but to save it.

At the same time, she knew exactly what he was feeling in not having the right clothes, and in a way it was worse for him than for her and Letty.

They had managed to appear original and spectacular the night before last, but it was something they could not do again. If they dined with the Earl tomorrow night as he had suggested, their gowns would be old-fashioned and she was quite sure that his penetrating eyes would not miss the fact.

She could understand how Anthony, like his father, wanted to enjoy himself and also cut a dash amongst the Bucks and Beaux, who, as well as the Dandies, were extremely conscious of their personal appearance.

She sighed despondently and thought how much better it would have been if Anthony had been able to finish his time at Oxford.

Then, if everything had gone well, their father had intended that he should go into the Horse Guards as he himself had done at the same age.

But now for Anthony to buy a commission in the

Household Cavalry was so impossible that it was not worth thinking about.

Then insidiously, almost as if the Devil were tempting her, Marista remembered the paintings in the Castle which nobody except the Earl's friend had realised were valuable.

'It is too late now, even if I wished to become a thief, which I have no intention of being,' she thought.

At the same time, she felt her whole being crying out against the injustice of the Earl gaining more than he had anticipated from the turn of a card, when it might have meant so much in so many ways to her family.

Then sharply, almost as if she called herself to attention, she stopped thinking about Anthony's problems and wondered what she could do about their unexpected guest.

Anthony had said he was English, but even so it would be a great mistake for Hannah or Letty to know where he had come from or to think that in any way there was something mysterious about him.

She considered the problem and decided it was wise of Anthony to insist that nobody outside the house should know he was there, since otherwise there would have to be explanations.

Nobody could arrive on the Stage-Coach without everybody in the village knowing about it. Because they had so little to think about, it was news if a chicken laid an extra egg or somebody's horse shed a shoe.

At the moment, Marista knew, they would be occupied in talking about the Earl and his party, so they could not expect that there would be any material for gossip from Dovecot House.

When Mr. Tolmarsh left, which Marista expected would be today, they would naturally think he had been staying at the Castle.

108

Then she remembered that none of the Earl's guests would travel by Stage-Coach, and so once again there was a problem, and it seemed that her mind was full of questions with no answers.

There was no point in getting up so early, but she knew she would not be able to sleep again, so she got out of bed and drew back the curtains.

She had been so tired last night after being late the previous evening that she had not heard the rain.

Now there was every evidence that there had been a severe storm.

The flowers in the garden were battered, there were pools on the paths, and the sunshine glittering on the wet petals made each one sparkle iridescently.

The sea was calm but there was a slight haze over it, which she thought would have helped to hide a boat slipping into the caves beneath the Castle just before dawn.

At the same time, she knew that Anthony had taken unnecessary risks, as had the local smugglers, in crossing the Channel in the summer.

It was much easier in the winter, when the nights were long and they could leave in the dark and return in the dark.

She was aware that this week there was a full moon, and that, she thought, could be a danger, until she remembered that the rain-clouds would have obscured its light and given them the cover they needed to reach England in safety.

"Thank You, God . . . for bringing Anthony safely back," Marista prayed. "But please, do not let him go again. Next time he might be . . . wounded . . . or even . . . killed."

It still nagged at her mind that Mr. Tolmarsh, whoever he might be, had paid an amazingly large sum for his passage.

'He must have been desperate,' Marista thought,

and decided that the reason must have been that he was terrified of being captured again by the French and taken back to prison.

That, she told herself, was one question answered, but there were still a great many more, and when finally she was dressed and went downstairs, it was to find Hannah in the kitchen, making herself a cup of tea.

"You're up early, Miss Marista!" Hannah exclaimed. "I thought you'd have a good sleep this morning."

Marista sat down at the kitchen-table.

"It is a lovely morning," she said, "and I expect the sun woke me."

"The rain kept me awake half the night," Hannah grumbled, "raining like cats and dogs, it was, and there're wet footsteps all over the Hall and up the stairs."

The way Hannah spoke told Marista that she knew who had been out in the storm last night, but because she loved Anthony perhaps best of all the family, his secret was safe with her.

Because she did not wish to discuss it, Marista said quickly:

"Sir Anthony brought a friend home to stay the night. We have put him in the attic-bedroom."

There was a pause before Hannah said:

"I put some blankets up there the other day, but there're no sheets on the bed."

"We can make it up properly if he stays another night," Marista said.

"Sir Anthony shouldn't be bringing his friends here without giving me warning," Hannah remarked, "and anyhow we can't afford guests."

Marista put the three sovereigns down on the table and Hannah stared at them as if she felt they were something evil. Then she said:

"Beggars can't be choosers, and money's money, wherever it comes from, but if she knew what was going on in this house, your poor mother'd turn in her grave!"

"I know," Marista said in a low voice, "but there is . . . nothing we can do . . . about it."

"When I sees His Lordship come here yesterday, walking in as if he owned the place and the whole world with it, I nearly gave him a piece of my mind!"

"Oh, Hannah, please do not upset him!" Marista pleaded. "I am hoping to persuade him not to charge us any rent."

"If he does," Hannah said, "I swear I'll curse him and his descendents with every curse any Witch or Warlock has ever used."

She spoke so violently that Marista gave a cry of protest.

"That is not like you, Hannah, and to curse any-body is wicked."

"If His Lordship turns us out of here like he turned us out of the Castle," Hannah answered, "then I can only hope he suffers every torment ever invented by Satan!"

Because Hannah sounded almost like a Witch herself and it was unusual for her to be so dramatic, Marista gave a little laugh.

Then she said:

"I have the dismal feeling, Hannah, that curses would just bounce off the Earl without hurting him, like water off a duck's back, and I am sure that to plead with him would be far more effective."

"Well, you try pleading with him, Miss Marista," Hannah said tartly, "and I'll do a bit of pleading with Master Anthony. He's got to think of us instead of himself, and if he gets into trouble and lands up in prison, where'll we be?"

"Don't upset him, Hannah," Marista begged. "I have tried to make him promise that this will be the last time."

She paused before she added:

"He has given us some money which will pay any bills we owe and ensure that we have food for a little while, at any rate."

"Tainted money!" Hannah said. "Those that bring it in will all be sitting in Church this morning, grinning like Cheshire cats at their cleverness, but one day they'll get their just reward!"

"No, do not say that!" Marista exclaimed. "I am sure it is unlucky!"

Hannah drank her tea, and Marista went from the kitchen to start dusting and tidying the small Sitting-Room, which was always one of her tasks.

Then she saw that thrown over a chair in the Hall was a coat.

She picked it up and realised it was very wet, and because she had never seen it before, she knew that it belonged to Anthony's guest.

She took it into the kitchen and said to Hannah:

"Can I hang this up over the stove? It is soaking wet and will take hours to dry outside."

"Give it to me," Hannah said. "You'd think there was enough work to do in this house without anybody bringing me any more!"

Hannah had arranged a cord and pulley over the top of the stove, on which they could hang things which had to be dried quickly.

It was extremely useful in the winter, when there was no sun outside to dry things on the line, but Marista felt sometimes that for things to be dried in this way made them smell of food, and she always avoided having anything she owned hung over the stove.

As Hannah spread out the coat before hanging it over the stove, Marista saw it was very French-looking in the way it was made. At the same time, the material was good, and it had a two-tiered cape over the shoulders.

This made it heavy, and as Hannah tried to pull the cord up, Marista helped her.

"I suppose I've got to put up with that dripping over my pots and pans!" Hannah grumbled.

As she spoke, a drip sizzled into the fire as if to prove her point, and Marista said placatingly:

"I hope it will not take long, and anyway when it is a little drier than it is now it can go out in the garden."

As the stranger's coat was so wet, she thought that whatever Anthony had been wearing would be the same, and the sooner they were dried, the better.

Without saying any more to Hannah, she went upstairs and along the passage where there were three bedrooms, one occupied by Letty, one by herself, and one by Anthony.

When her parents were alive, she and Letty had shared a room, and only after her father and mother were dead had she moved into the big room that she now occupied.

Hannah had a tiny room near the kitchen, and the only other bedroom in the house was in the small attic, where Anthony had put Mr. Tolmarsh.

Very quietly Marista opened the door of Anthony's bedroom and found, as she expected, that the clothes he had been wearing were all thrown down on the floor, while he himself lay fast asleep in bed.

Because he was always a sound sleeper there was really no risk of her waking him, but still she tiptoed to where his clothes lay, picked them up, and slipped out of the room, closing the door very quietly behind her.

She was walking along the passage holding the sodden garments in front of her so that they would not wet the gown she was wearing, when she heard somebody coming down the tiny narrow staircase from the attic.

She stopped, turned, and came face to face with Edward Tolmarsh.

He was dark, not very tall, and if Anthony had not already told her he was an Englishman, he might easily have been French.

"Good-morning!"

He bowed and added:

"I think you must be Miss Rockbourne."

"We will talk downstairs," Marista whispered, "because my sister and brother are both asleep."

"Yes, of course."

He stood back for her to pass him and she went ahead down the stairs, conscious that he was following her.

When she reached the Hall she said:

"If you will go into the Dining-Room, which is the room on the right, I will ask Hannah to prepare you some breakfast."

She did not wait to see if he obeyed her, but hurried to the kitchen with Anthony's clothes, which she placed on the floor in front of the stove, and said to Hannah:

"The gentleman who is staying with us is in the Dining-Room. Will you cook his breakfast while I lay the table?"

She then hurried back to the Dining-Room, where Mr. Tolmarsh was standing at the window looking out towards the sea.

"You must be very tired," Marista began, "and I am sure that Anthony will sleep until luncheon-time."

"Do not worry about me," he replied, "but I hope your brother has told you that no-one must know that I am here."

"Yes, he told me your necessity for secrecy," Marista agreed, "and from our point of view it is best that nobody should be aware of it, in case they ask how you . . . arrived."

Mr. Tolmarsh nodded his head. His eyes were on

Marista, and she thought he was staring at her in a somewhat embarrassing manner.

Because she wanted to be nice to him, she said:

"It must have been very upsetting for you and your family to have been prisoners of the French."

"It was a horrifying experience."

He spoke slowly, making each word seem a little drawn out, as if he would accentuate what he was saying.

"And what about your father and mother? Will they be able to escape too?" Marista asked.

Mr. Tolmarsh shook his head.

"It is impossible."

"Perhaps the war will not last very much longer. Then they will be able to join you in England."

"That is of course what they wish to do."

There was silence, and Marista wondered what else she could say to him.

"That big Castle," Mr. Tolmarsh said after a moment. "Who lives there?"

"My family used to live there," Marista replied, "but now it belongs to the Earl of Stanbrook."

Mr. Tolmarsh frowned.

"The Earl of Stanbrook? You are sure it is he who owns the Castle?"

"Yes, indeed. He is staying there now."

"He is staying at the Castle?"

"Yes, he came here two days ago."

Mr. Tolmarsh stared at her as if he did not believe her. Then he asked:

"We are talking of the Earl of Stanbrook, who is a great friend of His Royal Highness the Prince Regent, and whose horses win so many big races?"

"I think that is a very apt description of him!" Marista said, smiling.

"I had no idea," Mr. Tolmarsh said slowly, "that he

115

would be at that Castle. I thought he would be living in London."

"He owns the Castle and a great many other houses and Estates."

"Tell me about the Castle," Mr. Tolmarsh asked. "You say it once belonged to your family, so you must know it well."

"Very well," Marista agreed. "It is very old, having first been built in Norman times."

Mr. Tolmarsh seemed very interested and she told him the history of the Castle and how it had been added to by succeeding generations.

When Hannah came in with his breakfast, Mr. Tolmarsh went on talking about the Castle.

Hannah gave Marista only toast for breakfast, so she knew they were short of eggs, and when Mr. Tolmarsh asked if there was any more for him to eat, she told him politely that she was afraid the hens had not been very obliging at the moment.

Fortunately, there was enough butter and a pot of honey which Hannah had been given by the village Bee-Keeper.

Marista fancied that Mr. Tolmarsh looked somewhat disparagingly at the cottage-loaf, and she remembered her father saying that the French enjoyed *croissants* for breakfast.

However, they went on talking about the Castle, and finally when Marista rose to carry his plate and her own into the kitchen he said:

"Since I suppose it would be impossible to visit this beautiful Castle, I wonder if you have a book about it, or perhaps a map you could show me of how it was built."

Marista smiled.

"When we left the Castle, books written about the history of my family were amongst the things we brought away with us, and in several of them I know there are plans showing the Castle as it was in Norman times, and how century by century it developed into the large building it has become."

"How very interesting!" Mr. Tolmarsh exclaimed. "I would so much like to read of such development."

'He is obviously a student of history,' Marista thought to herself, 'and rather pedantic about it.'

However, she thought it would keep him interested, so she found a book and settled him down in the Sitting-Room before she went to the kitchen to help Hannah prepare luncheon before they went to Church.

"It looks as though there'll be no Church for me today!" Hannah complained crossly. "With an extra mouth to feed there's not enough for ourselves as it is."

"Shall I bring in some more vegetables from the garden?" Marista asked. "I am sure there are some new potatoes, and despite the rain there will be more peas than there were yesterday."

"You get yourself ready for Church, Miss Marista," Hannah said, "and I hope next time Master Anthony gets his clothes wet, it won't be on a Saturday night!"

"Or any other night," Marista said beneath her breath.

She had already realised that she would be the only one of the family to represent them in Church today, and as she went upstairs to put on her bonnet, she wondered if she should wake Letty, then decided against it.

She always grew bored with the Morning Service on Sundays when the Vicar insisted on preaching a long, rambling sermon to which nobody listened.

Evensong was much more lively and was attended by many more of the villagers.

Because her mother had always gone to Matins, Marista thought that was what she should do too, although the family pew in the Chancel, which was carved with the Rockbourne coat-of-arms, besides having comfortable velvet seats for them to sit on, seemed very empty with nobody else there.

Accordingly, she went off alone, feeling that she was being very virtuous, and only when she reached the Church did she wonder for the first time whether if the Earl was in residence they were entitled to sit in their own family pew.

Then she told herself that she was quite certain that none of his house-party would come to Church, and why she should be so sure of that was a question she could answer quite easily.

The shock of learning that Lord Dashford, although married, was trying to flirt with her, and that Anthony was enamoured of his wife, was still in her mind.

What she had seen of the rest of the Earl's guests told her that they were prepared to behave in very much the same way.

"The sooner they all leave, the better," she told herself as she walked through the lych-gate.

Then, because she could not help being honest with herself, Marista knew that everything would seem very flat and rather dull once the Earl returned to London.

The Church was only half-full and the congregation consisted mostly of very old people who would not turn out for Evensong. But the flowers on the Altar were lovely against the old stone.

The monuments and tombs to generations of Rockbournes seemed particularly moving this morning, and Marista had the strange feeling that they were welcoming her, aware that she needed their support.

The Vicar's wife played the organ, and Marista stepped into the family pew, closed the little carved-oak door behind her, and knelt down on the soft cassock that her mother had always used.

She prayed for quite a long time, thanking God that Anthony had returned safely from France and praying that the Earl would let them stay at Dovecot House without paying any rent.

Only when she rose from her knees to sit back on the seat was she aware that something unusual was happening in the Church.

She looked down the aisle and saw with surprise that the Earl was being escorted up the Chancel by the Vicar.

It flashed through her mind that because it was his first appearance since taking possession of the Castle, it was the correct thing for the Vicar to do.

At the same time, she was surprised that he was aware of it.

Then as they reached the top of the short aisle and the Vicar indicated the pew in which she was sitting, Marista realised that she was now an interloper in the place that had been hers ever since she could remember.

She wondered if she should get up and sit elsewhere. Then she realised that as the Earl was alone there was plenty of room, and if she moved away it might be interpreted in a different manner from what she intended.

Instead she sat still, thankful that she had not taken her father's place, which was a high-backed seat with arms and a raised shelf in front of him for his books.

Having shown the Earl to his place, the Vicar then crossed the aisle to his own seat and sank down in prayer.

The Earl merely covered his eyes for a moment, then sat back to look at Marista.

There was a faint smile on his lips, as if he knew she was surprised to see him, before he said in a voice that only she could hear:

"Good-morning, Marista! You see, I am doing my duty."

"I . . . I did not expect . . . you," Marista replied,

"and I am afraid I have only just realised that I should not sit . . . here, now that the Castle no . . . longer belongs to my family."

"I think we can at least share a pew," the Earl replied, "and there appears to be no pressure on the part of anybody else to join us."

She supposed that he was referring to his own house-party, and she whispered:

"Late nights and Church-going are not very compatible."

There was no chance to say any more, for the Vicar began the Service.

Perhaps because he was over-awed at having the Earl present, the Vicar preached more simply than usual, Marista thought, and, to her astonishment, for only ten minutes.

It was so surprising, since he was usually so long-winded, that she was sure the Earl had given him a time-limit.

The choir-boys for once behaved well, and although it was all very familiar to Marista, she was trying to see it through the Earl's eyes and was aware that it must seem an hour of boredom for him.

The congregation waited for them to leave first, as they had in her father's day.

As they walked out of the Church, down the path, and through the lych-gate, the Earl said:

"You can drive home with me. I came in style, as I thought you would expect me to do."

Marista could not help giving a little laugh as she replied:

"I was quite certain you would not appear, and I am sure it is an experience you will not wish to repeat."

"Nevertheless," the Earl replied, "I hope it is duly noted as a good mark in my favour."

"Do you really want good marks? I thought you were completely satisfied with yourself exactly as you are."

"That, I admit, is what I thought until I came to the Castle," the Earl replied. "Since then, Marista, you have pointed out my faults and defects so clearly that now I am very conscious of them."

Marista gave a little cry.

"Oh, I hope not! It would be a great mistake if you changed yourself! For good or bad . . . you are . . . you."

The Earl turned a little sideways in his seat so that he could look at her.

They were driving in a very comfortable open carriage, and Marista was very conscious of how smart and elegant he looked, wearing champagne-coloured pantaloons beneath his cut-away coat and Hessian boots which she was certain would make Anthony very envious.

His white cravat was an achievement all its own, and she thought a little despairingly that if that was how Anthony wished to look, the forty-five pounds he had left would not go very far.

"What is worrying you, Marista?" the Earl asked.

"How do you know I am . . . worried?"

"I have told you before that your eyes are very expressive."

"Then I shall have to keep them downcast when you are there, or speak only of things I . . . want you to . . . know."

"I have an idea, although I may be wrong," the Earl said, "that there are a great number of things you are hiding from me."

Because his remark took her by surprise, she asked quickly:

"Why should you . . . think I have . . . secrets?"

"Shall I say that my intuition tells me quite positively that you are hiding something that worries you."

It flashed through Marista's mind that there were a great number of things: Anthony's money, the friend he had brought to the house whom they must not talk

121

about, his involvement with Lady Dashford, and his insistence that he must go to London.

"Exactly!" the Earl said, as if she had spoken aloud. "Now, suppose you tell me about them and let me worry with you."

"No . . . no . . . of course not," Marista said. "One cannot talk about a . . . secret with . . . anybody."

"You are sure about that?"

"Quite sure!"

"I am disappointed," the Earl said. "I thought you trusted me."

"I do," Marista said, "but this is not concerning Lord Dashford."

As she spoke, she thought that was not quite true. Yet, how could she tell the Earl that Anthony was obtaining money by dangerous means just so that he could be with Lady Dashford in London?

The horses were drawing up outside Dovecot House, which was only a little way from the Church, and as they did so the Earl put out his hand and laid it on Marista's.

"I can always sense when you are worried," he said. "You should stop worrying about other people and think about yourself and your looks, as I advised you to do when we first met."

Fortunately, Marista did not have to answer him, for the carriage came to a standstill and the footman jumped down from the box to open the door.

"Good-bye, My Lord," she said, as he walked with her up the path to the front door, "and thank you very much for bringing me home."

"I think it is very inhospitable of you not to invite me in," the Earl remarked drily.

It was then that Marista realised that to do so could be disastrous.

She had left Mr. Tolmarsh in the Sitting-Room,

and for all she knew he was still there, reading the book about the Castle.

Because the Earl's suggestion frightened her, for a moment she could only stare at him, wondering what she should say. Then as she was aware that he was waiting, she said a little nervously:

"I . . . I am sorry . . . but this morning it is not . . . convenient for you to come in. Letty was asleep when I left, and she may . . . not be . . . dressed."

It all sounded very confused, and she thought the Earl was looking at her as if he knew that she was not only making excuses but was also frightened.

She feared he might argue with her, but after a moment he said:

"I would be very obtuse, Marista, if I did not realise that I was not welcome, but I shall look forward to seeing you tomorrow evening, if not before."

He swept his hat from his head, and Marista curtsied. Then he walked back to his carriage and she waited on the doorstep until he drove away.

However, he did not wave back at her as she had expected, but as the horses with their silver harness gleaming and glittering in the sunshine moved towards the Castle, she had the feeling that the Earl was angry with her.

"What else could I say?" she asked herself despairingly.

# Chapter Six

Marista walked across the Hall, and as she did so she heard voices in the Sitting-Room.

She realised that Anthony was downstairs talking to Mr. Tolmarsh, and as she paused for a moment she heard her brother say:

"When I was a boy I used to find it great fun to slip out at night after I had been put to bed, and of course there were dozens of ways of getting out of the Castle."

"What were they?" Mr. Tolmarsh asked.

Anthony paused. Marista knew he was thinking of the secret passages, and as he obviously could not mention those to a stranger, he replied:

"I think the easiest way was by one of the lower windows in the Norman Tower, which is almost on the edge of the cliff. Nobody worried if the shutters fitted there, which they did not, or noticed that the catch on the window was broken."

He laughed before he added:

"I was often afraid when it was dark that I would fall over the cliff and be drowned!"

Marista did not wait to hear any more.

She went to the kitchen and saw as she entered it that Hannah was busy at the stove, and that Mr. Tolmarsh's coat and other clothes were thrown over a chair in a far corner of the room.

"I am back, Hannah," she said. "Is Letty awake?"

"Awake and gone!" Hannah replied abruptly.

"Gone? Where?"

"Need you ask?" Hannah answered. "That young Lord was here asking for her before she had finished her breakfast, and she told me she would not be back for luncheon."

Marista gave a little sigh, thinking it was a mistake for Letty to spend so much time with Lord Lampton.

Then she knew it was a blessing in disguise, because it would put off the time when she would have to explain about Mr. Tolmarsh. Perhaps if she met him later in the day it would not seem so obvious that he had arrived during the night.

"Can I help you, Hannah?" Marista asked, knowing the old maid was in a bad temper.

"You can put those wet clothes out in the garden if you like," Hannah remarked. "They're making the whole kitchen steam, and Heaven knows when they'll be dry enough for anybody to wear them."

"The sun is hot now," Marista said, "and there is a slight wind. I will hang them on the line."

She picked them up as she spoke and carried them out through the kitchen door to the part of the garden where Hannah had hung a clothes-line.

It was easy to peg Anthony's clothes onto it, but she knew Mr. Tolmarsh's coat was so heavy that it would sag down nearly to the ground.

Therefore, having left the coat until last, she threw it over the low wall on which there were some small plants which had not yet come into flower.

She hoped the coat would not crush them too badly, but there was nowhere else where it could get the sun.

As it struck the bricks there was a strange sound, and she thought in consternation that she must have broken something in one of the pockets.

She hoped it was not a watch or anything else that was made of glass, and because she was worried, she felt tentatively in the pockets, hoping there was nothing that would cut her fingers.

The two pockets on the outside of the coat were empty, yet she definitely had heard the sound of something striking the bricks.

She opened the coat and looked for an inside pocket and found just over the breast an opening which had been stitched rather untidily.

In fact, it was so roughly done that she thought to herself that whoever had sewn it had been a man, perhaps Mr. Tolmarsh himself.

She felt round it and was certain that something was in it.

It did not seem like a watch, but she could not be sure because the coat was made of such thick material and the lining was a stiff satin.

Without really thinking whether it was right or wrong for her to do so, she pulled open the stitching, which she told herself was only the most amateurish form of sewing, and slipped her hand inside.

She felt something hard and metallic, and pulling it out she found that it was not a watch as she had feared, but a long knife which looked like an Italian stiletto such as her father had often described to her.

There was a piece of paper wrapped round it, and the point of it was embedded in a small cork.

She knew then that she had been needlessly alarmed that she had broken anything, because the stiletto was very strongly made, and she knew that Mr. Tolmarsh must have brought it with him as a weapon with which to defend himself when he was escaping from France.

As she looked at it Marista's imagination began to work, and she felt that in some way it must have been smuggled into the prison where he was interned with his father and mother.

Perhaps, because he had been so desperate to escape, he had been obliged to kill one of the guards with it before he climbed over the prison-wall and started on the long journey from France to England.

Carried away by her own imagination, she stood in the sun, looking down at the stiletto, then realised that she was intruding on Mr. Tolmarsh's privacy, which was something she should not do.

She thought that if she put it back into the pocket perhaps he would not realise that she had broken the threads, and she might have time to mend them later when the coat was dry.

She started to wrap the piece of paper back round the stiletto in the way she had found it, when she saw that there was something written on it.

A name jumped out at her, and without really thinking she read what was written:

> THE PRINCE REGENT
> VISCOUNT PALMERSTON
> VISCOUNT MELVILLE
> THE EARL OF STANBROOK

Quickly, because she felt that the list was not for her eyes, Marista wrapped the paper round the stiletto and put it back into the pocket from which she had taken it.

Then she spread the coat out a little farther in the sunshine and walked back into the house.

Later, when she had gone upstairs to her bedroom and taken off her bonnet and changed what was her best gown, in which she had gone to Church, for a more simple, everyday one, she wondered why Mr. Tolmarsh had a list of such important people together with the stiletto in his coat.

Then with a faint smile she told herself that if those were the English friends he wished to contact now that he had returned to his own country, he was certainly aiming high.

She went downstairs to help carry the rabbit-stew, which smelt delicious, into the Dining-Room, and with it a dish of potatoes and another of green peas.

When she looked at the stew Marista did not say anything, but she thought there seemed very little for two grown men and perhaps it was a good thing that Letty was having luncheon at the Castle.

At the same time, she could not help feeling that the Earl would think it very pushy that she had gone there without his invitation and only because Lord Lampton had asked her.

'He is cross with me anyway, and perhaps this will make him crosser,' she thought, and wondered why the idea of his anger felt like a heavy stone in her breast and took away her appetite.

However, Anthony and Mr. Tolmarsh ate everything that was on the table.

Marista sensed that their guest missed being offered wine, which she supposed he was used to in France even in prison. But he said nothing and only sipped rather disdainfully the glass of water which was all they could provide.

There was a gooseberry tart to follow, but naturally no cream, because they could not afford to buy enough milk to stand in a big open bowl like those which had covered one of the cool slabs at the Castle when they had lived there.

Anthony did not seem to notice, and Marista thought that because she had had such delicious food the other evening and when she had picnicked yesterday with the Earl, she was now missing the little luxuries which in the old days she had taken entirely for granted.

"What are you going to do this afternoon?" she asked Anthony.

"Rest," he replied, and he yawned as he spoke.

"I would like you to tell me more about the Castle," Mr. Tolmarsh said. "I find it very interesting."

"It will have to wait until I can keep my eyes open!" Anthony replied. "And if we are going to London tomorrow, you will want to feel fresh and ready to enjoy yourself when you get there."

There was a little pause before Mr. Tolmarsh said:

"I may not go tomorrow, but perhaps the next day—it depends."

Marista gave her brother a frantic glance, knowing he would understand that it was difficult not only to keep Mr. Tolmarsh's presence a secret but that it was also an embarrassment from the housekeeping point of view.

Even though Hannah had some money, they would have to be very careful not to spend it too quickly.

Anthony, however, was looking not at her but at Edward Tolmarsh.

"I want to go to London," he said insistently, "but I can hardly leave you alone with my sisters."

"Then of course I must do my best to come with you," Mr. Tolmarsh replied.

Marista gave a little sigh of relief, and Anthony rose from the table and started to walk up the stairs.

She knew that ordinarily he would have gone to the Sitting-Room and slept comfortably on the sofa, but because he did not want to be disturbed by their guest, he was going to his own room.

Mr. Tolmarsh looked at Marista.

"I wonder, Miss Rockbourne," he said, "if you would have time to explain to me this plan of the Castle which I have been studying. It is very complicated and a little difficult to understand."

"Are you interested in Norman Castles?"

"I do not remember ever seeing one before," Mr. Tolmarsh replied slowly, "and certainly not one which is as beautiful as the one in which you once lived."

"I like to hear you say that."

She smiled, and as she did so she realised that he was not looking at her, but was staring down at the book he had brought with him into the Dining-Room.

She now realised that he had put it under his chair while they were eating, almost as if he was afraid it would vanish if he left it in the Sitting-Room.

She thought as she looked at him that there was something about him she did not like, but she could not understand what it was.

She was always conscious of the vibrations that came from people, and now because she was seeing him as a person for the first time, rather than as an encumbrance that had been thrust upon them by Anthony, she decided he was unpleasant in a manner which she could not explain.

She certainly had no wish to talk to him or to be close to him as she would be if they studied the plan together.

Impulsively, in the sort of way Letty would have spoken, she said:

"I am sorry, I am afraid you will have to wait for Anthony to wake up. I have so many things to do at the moment that I cannot stop to talk."

She thought Mr. Tolmarsh was going to expostulate with her, but she picked up the dirty plates and carried them into the kitchen.

After she had helped Hannah with the washing-up, she did not go to her own room but instead walked down on the beach.

She knew there would be nobody there, and it was somewhere she seldom went because it reminded her too vividly of her father.

Even now as she walked along the sands it was hard not to look out to sea, thinking that perhaps by some miracle she would see his dark head swimming back towards the shore.

"Oh, Papa," she said to herself, "if only you had stayed and not left us as you did. Perhaps, knowing the Earl, you could have come to some arrangement with him, and things would not have been so bad as they are now."

She told herself that the Earl had been very pleasant this morning until she had upset him, and she was almost certain that he would not turn them out of Dovecot House.

'I wish Papa had gone to see him when we first moved,' she thought, 'and told him the desperate straits in which we found ourselves.'

Then she knew that her father would never have humiliated himself more than he had been already.

It was the pride of the Rockbournes which had made him face death rather than plead with the Earl for indulgence.

"I suppose I should have pride too," Marista murmured. "But I have not only myself to think about, but Letty and Anthony."

She walked on, and now she was praying that the Earl would help her and allow them to stay at the house, and perhaps, in some way she could not quite determine, he would find a better job for Anthony than the one he had at the moment.

Perhaps he would think it an humiliation to be in the Earl's employment, but if it was a post of some authority and with a better salary, she was sure that she could persuade Anthony to accept it.

Then she began to worry about the trouble he might get into in London and how much she disliked the idea of his flirting with Lady Dashford.

Supposing Lord Dashford should be incensed and challenge Anthony to a duel?

Because so many possibilities were frightening her, she felt as if she must run away from them and, like her father, never come back.

\*   \*   \*

When Anthony came downstairs for tea, which Marista had arranged in the Dining-Room, there was nothing but the remains of the loaf of bread they had had for breakfast and the same comb of honey.

But Hannah had made a few warm scones, and both Anthony and Mr. Tolmarsh ate them with relish.

There was still no sign of Letty, and Marista went into the kitchen to ask Hannah what they were having for dinner.

"Vegetable soup and a small omelette. There's nothing else, so there's no use asking for it."

"Shall I go to the farm and buy some more eggs for an omelette?" Marista enquired.

"Guests must take what they can get in this house," Hannah said. "If the gentleman doesn't like what we serve him, then he knows the answer."

"That is not very hospitable, Hannah," Marista protested.

"Master Anthony should know better than to ask people here without giving me any warning," Hannah replied tartly. "I know he's produced some money, and I don't like to think how it was come by, but Sunday is Sunday, and I'm not shopping on the Sabbath, not even for the King of England himself!"

Marista wanted to laugh at the way Hannah was speaking, but she knew she must keep a straight face.

"I'm now going to Church!" Hannah said firmly. "If Miss Letty were here I'd make her come with me. As it is, I'll go on my own."

As she spoke, she put on her plain black bonnet and a woollen shawl round her shoulders, then picked up her black cotton gloves and her prayer-book from the dresser.

She did not say any more, but the way she shut the back door sounded very much like a slam.

Marista knew that Hannah was upset over what

Anthony had done last night and at the way Letty was behaving.

She was so much a part of the family that their troubles were her troubles, and Marista knew that Hannah instinctively disliked Mr. Tolmarsh as much as she did.

'All the same,' she thought, 'he has to eat, and at least I can get more vegetables from the garden.'

It took her a little time to dig up some potatoes, to pull the carrots, which were still very small, and to find a cabbage that had not been eaten by the pigeons which were an unending nuisance.

She washed them all and left them ready for Hannah when she returned. Then, because she too felt tired after having been awake so early in the morning, she went upstairs to lie on her bed.

She did not read the book she was halfway through, but instead she must have dozed off, because she awoke with a start as the door opened and Letty came in.

"You are back, Letty!" Marista exclaimed.

"Did I wake you? I'm sorry."

"No, no, I am awake. Have you had a nice time?"

"Wonderful, wonderful!" Letty cried. "I have never had such a happy day!"

The way she spoke and the sudden radiance in her face told Marista that her sister was in love.

She had only to look at her and to hear the lilt in her voice to know that what she feared had happened. Letty was in love with Lord Lampton, and she wondered wildly what she could say to her.

"I cannot stay talking," Letty said before Marista could speak. "I have to change very quickly. Peregrine is coming to fetch me at seven-thirty."

"Fetch you?" Marista repeated stupidly.

"I am dining at the Castle. I will tell you all about it tomorrow."

"But, Letty . . . I must . . ." Marista began, but Letty put up her hands.

"No, no, Marista, do not spoil it. I know exactly what you are going to say, and I could not bear it at the moment."

As she spoke she slipped out of the room, and Marista sank back despairingly against her pillows, thinking that things were far worse than she had anticipated.

Because she was so distressed and worried about Letty, she went up to bed almost immediately after dinner, feeling that she could not listen to Mr. Tolmarsh talking in his slow, boring voice to Anthony.

However, before she left she drew her brother aside to say:

"Are you going to London tomorrow, or not?"

"Of course I am going, if I can make Tolmarsh come with me," Anthony replied. "He is being tiresome. He keeps saying perhaps he will have to stay another day, and I cannot understand why."

"The Stage-Coach does not go until eleven o'clock," Marista said. "I presume you have told Farmer Dawson that you will not be working for him for the next few days?"

Anthony grinned.

"As a matter of fact I had forgotten," he said. "I will go and tell him right away. He will be quite decent about it. He always is."

Marista kissed her brother's cheek.

"Good-night," she said. "I will see you in the morning."

"Good-night, Marista," Anthony said. "I am sorry about Tolmarsh. At the same time, I am delighted to have his money. I have left ten pounds for you and Letty in the drawer in my bedroom, and I have given Hannah what I promised her for the housekeeping."

"I am sure she is pleased to have it."

"She grabbed it, at the same time giving me a lecture."

They both laughed. Then Marista went up to bed, trying not to think of the money that Hannah had said was tainted.

It was some time before she fell asleep.

Then she awoke, knowing that she had been asleep for hours and wondering what had disturbed her.

As she did so she was aware of very, very soft footsteps moving past her door.

For a moment she thought she was mistaken. Then, because the floor-boards always creaked, she knew that somebody was going down the stairs and wondered if it was Anthony, feeling hungry after such a light dinner and looking in the kitchen for something to eat.

She knew that if he ate what Hannah had decided was for breakfast, everybody else would go hungry.

She was just thinking that she had better get up early and, if the hens had not laid enough eggs, fetch some from the farm, when she heard the bolt on the front door being pulled back.

She had said weeks ago that the bolt needed oiling, but needless to say they had had no oil.

She wondered now why Anthony was going out-of-doors. Then it struck her that perhaps it was not Anthony but Mr. Tolmarsh, although why such a thought should come to her mind she had no idea.

She slipped out of bed, went to the window, and pulled aside the curtains, and was instantly aware that the moon, which was three-quarters full, was shining with a silver light and transforming everything it touched into a mystical loveliness.

She looked down and saw Mr. Tolmarsh moving through the little wooden gate and onto the dusty roadway.

She wondered where he was going and saw with surprise that he was wearing his overcoat, which Hannah had brought in and laid on a chair in the Hall just before dinner when it was growing dark.

It was so warm that it seemed strange that Mr. Tolmarsh should need an overcoat, although perhaps, Marista thought, if he lived in France he was not as impervious to the cold of England as Anthony was, and, she was sure, the Earl.

She watched him moving a little way up the road before he left it to walk across the rough grass which led towards the drive.

Then for the first time a thought came to her which was so startling and so horrifying that she held her breath.

She suddenly realised as if it were written in letters of fire why Mr. Tolmarsh, if that was his name, had come to England, why he carried a stiletto secretly in his pocket, and why four names were inscribed on the paper in which it was wrapped.

Then as she thought of it she blamed herself for having been very stupid, so stupid that she could hardly believe she had not thought of it before.

Viscount Palmerston was the Secretary of War, Viscount Melville was the First Lord of the Admiralty, and the Earl was not only the most famous race-horse owner in England but was closely connected with Members of the Government and of course the Prince Regent.

At the thought of the Prince's name at the top of the list, Marista gave a little gasp of sheer horror and started frantically to dress herself.

As she did so she knew that she had not only to save the Earl from being killed by a French spy, but she must also save the Prince Regent, and of course Anthony, who had inadvertently brought their murderer into the country.

She flung on the first gown she could find, pulled a shawl over her shoulders, and without arranging her hair or looking at herself in the mirror she ran down the stairs and out through the front door.

However, she did not take the same route as Mr. Tolmarsh had, but set off along the lower side of the Park, which led directly into the Castle garden.

She would have known her way blindfolded, but the fact that the moon was shining so brightly made it easier, and if by any chance he was looking to see if he was being watched or followed, there were shrubs and trees to conceal her.

Although he had a good start, she knew that while he had studied the plans of the Castle and picked Anthony's brains as to how he could enter it, he had not the advantage she had of being able to use one of the secret passages to reach the man he intended to assassinate.

Marista had not thought to look at the clock before she left Dovecot House, but she reckoned it must be between one and two o'clock in the morning, and the Earl would be in bed.

As she hurried along, running wherever she could, she thought that Mr. Tolmarsh, being very persistent, would undoubtedly have learnt, from the plan in the book or from Anthony, which was the Master-Bedroom.

It was there that all the owners of the Castle had slept, and it was redolent with the history of which they were so proud.

Kings who had visited the Castle had always slept in the great bedroom which adjoined on one side of the Northern Tower and on the other side the older State-Rooms.

Some of these had been built after the Restoration of Charles II and some by later owners of the Castle, including her grandfather.

They were all very impressive, but most impressive of all was the bedroom which her father had loved, with the canopy of its great four-poster bed carved and embellished with the Rockbourne coat-of-arms and their motto.

That was where Mr. Tolmarsh would be seeking the Earl to kill him with the stiletto she had held in her hands and which she knew could pierce a man through the heart with one single stroke, so that he would die instantly.

The mere idea of it made her run on again until she was breathless. Then as she twisted her way through the great bushes of lilac and syringa, she entered one of the ancient gardens that had been laid out centuries earlier.

In it there was an arbour, now completely obscured by honeysuckle, where, if one knew where to look, was one of the entrances to the secret passages.

It was not the Normans who had built the secret passages at Rock Castle but the Protestants who were seeking to escape from the persecutions of Mary Tudor.

Then when for a short time the Rockbourne of the day was converted to Roman Catholicism, it was Jesuits who fled from being hung or drawn and quartered under the laws of Queen Elizabeth.

Her father had always told Marista that they had added quite a number of the passages which honeycombed the Castle.

Later again in its history it became the one safe hiding-places on the coast for the Royalists.

Cromwellian troops ransacked the Castle and searched it time after time, but the passages kept their secrets, and the caves that were later used by smugglers safely concealed many men loyal to Charles Stuart before they crossed the Channel to join him in France.

Because Anthony and Marista were so close to each other, when he learnt from his father the secrets of the Castle, he broke an age-old tradition by showing his sister where they were.

To Marista it was the most intriguing, exciting

thing she could imagine, first to be able to disappear when she wanted to, secondly to be able to leave the Castle without anybody being aware of it, and thirdly to be able to peep in many rooms without anybody in them being aware that they were being overheard or seen.

"Thank you, God," she said now, "that Anthony was brave enough to tell me. Otherwise, if the Earl is found dead tomorrow and suspicion rests on the French spy, which it might easily do, Anthony will be implicated and perhaps taken to the Tower for interrogation."

She could easily see how it could happen, and how if he was proved guilty of being an accessory to murder, and of being a smuggler as well, he would be either hanged or transported.

The idea made her frantic to reach the Earl, and although logically her mind told her that the Frenchman could not get into the Castle as easily and as quickly as she could, she was still afraid.

It was nearly three years since she had last used any of the secret passages, and even then she had not used this particular one.

Pushing aside the honeysuckle that seemed to be fighting against her, she found the catch which opened the door at the back of the arbour.

Then there was the dark and the smell of damp earth, which she remembered.

She shut the door behind her and now she was in complete darkness except for small pin-points of light that had been skilfully contrived all the way along the passages.

Sometimes they were so tiny that they were of little use, but they were still there, and when there was a moon as there was tonight, they were like fireflies pointing the way.

The ground was soft under her feet and she could move quickly until she reached the first flight of steps.

Then she was obliged to go a little more slowly, rising and moving to another level, then rising again. Then, when she was inside the Castle, she went up stairs that were very narrow and yet wide and high enough for a man to walk without lowering his head.

She climbed and climbed until she reached what she knew was the centre of the Castle, where a number of other passages led off in different directions.

Here the streaks of moonlight coming in through the pin-points were longer, and it was easier to breathe.

She took the left-hand fork, moving, as she knew, on the same level as the State-Bedrooms towards the Master-Suite.

She knew when she passed the room which had been her mother's and which had been used by every chatelaine of the Castle.

Then there was a Sitting-Room, and Marista could remember it fragrant with flowers and filled with some of the loveliest children's pictures of their ancestors because her mother liked to be surrounded by them.

The passage came to an end and she knew as she reached out her hand that she was touching the wall of the Master-Bedroom.

By this time she was so breathless that she had to stand still for a moment and breathe deeply before she could proceed any farther.

Her heart was beating frantically, and because she was so afraid, she listened in case she could hear a cry of agony and know that she was too late and the spy had struck to kill.

Then she told herself that if he had followed what Anthony had told him, he would be creeping round the outside of the Norman Tower, which was quite a distance from where she was now.

With fingers that trembled and were very cold, she

searched for the catch which would open the door in the panelling which covered the walls of the room in which her father had always slept.

Because she was so nervous, for the moment she could not find it, then her finger touched metal and there was a very faint sound as the panel swung open.

For a moment she felt she dare not look, then she was aware that if the Earl was in bed, as she expected, because it was a hot night, he would have pulled back the curtains in front of the open windows.

The moonlight was streaming in brilliant and silver, illuminating the huge bed at the far end of the room.

However, she could not see if there was anybody in it, and drawing in her breath she stepped through the panel and into the bedroom.

It seemed to her absolutely silent, and it flashed through her mind like a streak of pain that perhaps the Earl was not here, and if he was in another part of the Castle it might be impossible to find him.

Then as she reached the side of the bed she could see the outline of his body under the counterpane and his head against the pillows.

He was alive and he was asleep.

She put out her hand, and yet when she would have touched him it fell to her side, and instead she said in a voice that trembled:

"My . . . Lord! My . . . Lord!"

The Earl stirred instantly and opened his eyes.

He looked up, saw her silhouetted against the moonlight, and stared incredulously, as if he thought he was dreaming or seeing a vision.

"Marista!"

The name seemed to be jerked from between his lips before he asked:

"What are you doing here? What is the matter?"

For a moment Marista felt as if she could not answer him.

Then in a voice that did not sound like her own she said:

"There is a . . . French spy . . . he is . . . entering the Castle to . . . kill you!"

The Earl sat up in bed and put his hand up to his forehead to push his hair into place, as if trying to convince himself that what he was hearing was real.

"What are you saying?" he asked.

His voice was low, as if he understood the need for secrecy.

"There is a spy . . . I cannot explain how . . . but he is here . . . he is climbing into the Castle . . . I think by the lower room in the Tower which faces the cliffs. It is easy to open the shutter because the . . . catch on the window is . . . broken. Once he is in, he will come up the . . . side-staircase which leads to this floor, and he will attempt to . . . kill you."

She expected the Earl to ask her a lot of questions. Instead, he said:

"Thank you, Marista. Now go to the window and stand with your back to me while I dress!"

It was an order, and because he was so firm about it Marista obeyed him.

She was still trembling and it was hard to breathe, but as she heard the Earl moving quickly about the room, she knew that he had taken her terror from her and that she felt quite confident that he would save both himself and everybody else involved in this terrible plot.

She heard him shut the wardrobe door before he said:

"Now I will go and find this man, and you are to stay here until I come back."

Marista did not question the command, but merely went towards him to say:

"Be . . . careful! Be very . . . very careful. He

has a . . . stiletto which is very sharp, and if it . . . pierces your heart, you will . . . die!"

"I understand," the Earl said, "and I will be careful."

He had his back to the moonlight, and she thought he smiled as he said:

"Leave this to me. Just do as I tell you, and do not be afraid. But pray, as I expect you will anyway."

"You know I . . . will," Marista replied, "and God go with . . . you."

She was not certain that he had heard her, because before she had finished speaking the door had closed softly behind him and she was alone.

She listened as if she could hear him leave, then knew that it was pointless to do so.

This part of the Castle was very strongly built, and in places the walls were four feet thick. She was also sure that just as the Earl had recarpeted the part of the Castle she had seen when she came to dinner, he would have laid the same thick-pile carpet down on the passage outside his room, and doubtless the staircase which led to the lower floor.

She walked to the window, but she knew even as she did so that from the Master-Bedroom it was impossible to see the Tower which adjoined it.

Instead, there was a magnificent view over the gardens, the Park, and part of the coast with its white jagged cliffs.

However, it was difficult to see anything at the moment, because the moonlight was on her face, and after a little while she went back to the bed and sat down on it.

Because it was so familiar and because in this room she felt very close to her father and mother, she found herself telling them of the difficulties she faced—her anxiety for Letty, for Anthony, and for the future without money or security.

Then, as if she felt she should be thinking not of

herself but of the Earl, she prayed that he would be safe and that Mr. Tolmarsh would not hurt him.

It seemed impossible to think that he might kill anybody so magnificent as the Earl of Stanbrook.

But Marista had not missed the fact that the door was unlocked, and it would have been quite easy for him to slip quietly into the room, as she had done, and stab the Earl while he slept.

In the morning it would have been impossible for anybody to guess who his assassin could be, because nobody was aware that there was a stranger from across the Channel staying at Dovecot House.

The implications of it all were very obvious, and now Marista was praying frantically that the Earl would be victorious in this as in everything else he undertook.

It seemed to her that she must have waited for hours or a century of time, but she was still praying when the door opened, and as she turned her head she saw in the moonlight the Earl coming in.

He looked so strong, and she knew without his even telling her that everything was all right.

It was as if his vibrations went out towards her and touched hers.

As she started to her feet, clasping her hands together with the intensity of her feelings, there was really no need for him to say quietly:

"He will not trouble us again."

Marista drew in her breath, and the Earl came close to her to look down at her, at her hair falling over her shoulders, her eyes dark and very large in the moonlight as she lifted her face to his.

"He is dead," he said, as if he thought she had not understood.

"You . . . killed . . . him?"

Her voice trembled, but her heart was singing.

"I killed him," the Earl confirmed, "and I have thrown him over the cliff into the sea. The tide will carry him away, and there is no reason for anybody to connect him with this Castle, with me, or with you, Marista."

He heard the deep sigh that seemed to come from the very depths of her heart before he asked:

"Who else knows that this man was in England?"

Because she had to tell him the truth, Marista replied:

"Only . . . Anthony and Hannah. I do not think Letty was aware that he was . . . in the house."

"That makes things easy," the Earl said. "You will say nothing to anybody, and I will come and talk to you tomorrow."

Because everything was better than Marista had dared to hope, she could only stare at him, her hands still clasped as if she were praying.

He looked down at her, and after a moment he said:

"I realise you came here via the secret passages and you must obviously return the same way. Do you want me to come with you?"

"No . . . no . . . I am . . . all right."

"Then go home," the Earl said, "and forget what has happened. And thank you, Marista, for saving my life."

As he spoke he put his arms round her and pulled her gently against him.

Again gently, almost as if he were kissing a child, his lips found hers.

For a moment she could hardly believe it was happening. Then she felt her whole body quiver, but it was different from the fear that had made her tremble.

The strength of the Earl's arms and his lips against hers gave her a feeling that she had never known before, but it was part of the moonlight, the Castle, the fragrance of the flowers, and everything she loved.

It was all there, and he gave it to her, and she felt

as if her whole body responded to him and became a part of him.

It was so wonderful, so mysterious, so perfect that she knew it could not be real and she was only imagining it.

Yet, for the moment it was a rapture that she had not believed possible, an ecstasy that she knew she had sought in her prayers and was Divine.

Then, before she could begin to grasp what was happening or to feel that her heart was moving from her breast into her lips, the Earl set her free.

"Go home, Marista," he said in a strange voice. "You are quite safe. There will be no more horrors to frighten you tonight."

Because it was almost impossible for her to move or to think, he helped her through the panel. As he took his hands from her, he shut the door behind her.

For a moment she could not move.

Then as if she walked in a dream she started to go very, very slowly down the steps that she had climbed so hurriedly only a short time before, guided by the little pin-points of light which seemed to be magnified until they enveloped her with the celestial glory of the angels.

Only when she stepped out into the arbour, and there was the scent of honeysuckle whose flowers and leaves touched her face, did she realise that she was not in a dream but on her way back to Dovecot House.

The moonlight seemed a part of the Earl, his arms, and his lips, and as she walked between the lilac bushes, finding her way instinctively rather than by thought, she knew that this was love.

She loved him until he filled the whole world, the sky, and the sea, and she knew that she had given her heart, now and for all eternity, to the Earl of Stanbrook.

# Chapter Seven

Marista awoke with an irrepressible feeling of happiness, then as she opened her eyes she remembered that it had been long after dawn before she fell asleep.

She had lain in her bed, feeling that the whole world was enchanted because the Earl had kissed her, and she thought now that when she had fallen asleep she had gone on dreaming about him, feeling that his arms were still round her and his lips were still on hers.

Then, slowly and insidiously, like a tide coming in to the shore, she came out of her dream-world and into reality.

First, she knew she would have to tell Anthony what had happened, and that was going to be very difficult because she would have to admit to him that the Earl knew he had brought a spy into the country.

As she thought of her brother she had a sudden fear that he might already have left for London and she would not see him.

Then she remembered that he would be aware that the so-called Edward Tolmarsh was not there, and presumably would not leave without asking her what had happened to him.

She was surprised that he had not awakened her,

because she was quite certain it was late in the morning, although nobody had come near her.

'There is also Letty to cope with,' she thought with a little throb of her heart.

She was afraid that for Letty to hear what she must know would leave her hurt, unhappy, and more miserable here than she had ever been.

Marista knew now that she would understand better than she could have done before exactly what Letty would suffer, because she would be feeling the same.

The Earl had kissed her and it had been the most wonderful thing that had ever happened. He had drawn her heart from her body and made it his, and to her the future would never be the same.

Yet, she told herself she had to be sensible about this.

It was the first time she had been kissed, but to the Earl she was only another woman to whom he had brought the wonder and glory of love. To him it had meant little and in time would mean nothing.

He had kissed her last night because he was thanking her for saving his life and was elated at disposing of a spy. Not only had he saved himself, but he had also struck a blow against the tyrant of Europe, Napoleon Bonaparte, who had been menacing the safety of England for fifteen years.

"He was grateful to me," Marista whispered, "but there was nothing very personal about it, and when he returns to London he will forget me."

She felt as if the stiletto which Mr. Tolmarsh would have used had struck her in the heart, and because she could not bear her thoughts any longer, she slipped out of bed to pull back the curtains.

The sun was golden, making the sea shimmer dazzlingly, but Marista looked towards the Castle, and almost as if the Earl could hear her she said softly:

"I love you . . . and although it will mean . . . nothing to . . . you, I shall go on . . . loving you . . . all my life."

She knew what she felt for him was what her mother had felt for her father, and he for her, and for the first time she could understand exactly why her mother had no wish to go on living in a world which did not hold the man she loved.

Love! Love! Love!

It was impossible to think of anything else, as Marista dressed herself and went to the dressing-table to sweep back her hair into a shining chignon and pin it into place.

As she looked in the mirror she saw not her own reflection but the faces of the ladies who had sat on either side of the Earl at dinner when she had dined at the Castle.

They had been so beautiful, so polished, so sophisticated, and although he had seemed bored with them, at the same time they belonged to his world, and he to theirs.

It was an inexpressible agony to think that soon the Castle would be closed again and it would be perhaps two years or more before the Earl returned.

"In the meantime, I have to look after us all," Marista chided herself, "and stop . . . crying for the moon."

She went downstairs and only as she reached the Hall did she see the time on the old grandfather-clock whose oak case was so dilapidated that it had not been worth selling when they had disposed of everything else.

She stared at it incredulously, thinking it could not be true that the hands pointed to noon and she had slept so late.

Hurriedly she ran to the kitchen to find Hannah.

"Why did you not wake me?" she asked.

"Master Anthony had orders that you were not to be woken," Hannah replied.

Marista stared at her as if she felt she could not have heard her correctly.

"What do you mean . . . had orders?"

"A note arrived by a groom from the Castle."

Marista was very still.

"For Anthony? What did it say?"

"I took it up to him," Hannah replied, "but when he read it he didn't tell me what it contained."

Her voice was sharp, as if she resented Anthony's secrecy, and she went on:

"He just said you were not to be woken and that he was going to the Castle immediately."

Marista clasped her hands together.

This meant that the Earl intended to tell Anthony what had happened, and she wondered if he would be very angry with him for bringing a spy into the country.

She felt as if her brain and the whole kitchen were whirling round her, and without thinking she sat down on one of the hard kitchen-chairs.

"That's not all," Hannah said in an uncompromising voice. "Miss Letty was fetched again about an hour ago by the young Lord, and there's something going on between those two that's got me worried."

"I am worried too," Marista managed to say. "Oh, Hannah, if he . . . breaks Letty's . . . heart . . . what are we to . . . do?"

"There's nothing we can do," Hannah answered. "If you ask me, all men are a nuisance and the world'd be a much better place without them!"

She spoke very crossly, and Marista knew she was upset, but there was nothing she could say because to go on talking only made everything seem worse.

She left the kitchen and went into the Sitting-Room.

The flowers needed water, and she thought vaguely in a part of her mind which was functioning apart from her worries that she should go out and pick some of the roses that were coming into bud.

Yet it all seemed too much effort, and she went to the casement window which Hannah would have opened earlier in the morning, and stood staring blindly out into the garden, thinking of the Earl.

Because he was so vivid in her mind, because even to think of him made the rapture he had evoked in her rise again into her breast, when she heard the door open she turned her head and was not really surprised to see him there.

He seemed even larger and more overpowering than she remembered, and he filled not only the room but her heart and the whole world.

She could not move, she could only stand in the sunshine, looking at him, and it seemed for the moment as if he too were turned to stone.

Then he shut the door behind him and asked:

"You are rested?"

Because she was bemused by his looks, by his very presence, and by the love which seemed to make her heart turn somersaults in her breast, she found it difficult to understand what he was saying.

Then, knowing he must be thinking her very stupid, she said:

"Yes . . . yes . . . of course."

The Earl walked across the room to stand with his back to the fireplace.

"I want to talk to you, Marista," he said. "Come and sit down."

She obeyed him, moving slowly towards the armchair on the hearth-rug, and when she was seated in it the Earl sat down opposite her.

His eyes were on her face, and because he made her feel shy she looked away from him as she asked:

151

"You . . . are not . . . angry with . . . Anthony?"

"I sent for him for a different reason," the Earl replied, "and that is what I have to tell you."

Because she was frightened at what she was about to hear, Marista's eyes widened and there was a look of fear in their grey depths.

"I have had a long talk with your brother," he began, "and I have suggested to him that he should enter the Household Cavalry in which his father served, and spend at least three to four years in the Army before he returns to civilian life."

Marista drew in her breath. Then she said:

"Do you really . . . mean what you are . . . saying? But . . . how can Anthony . . . afford it?"

"Because you have made me so very conscious," the Earl replied, and she thought his eyes were twinkling, "of the pride of the Rockbournes, I pointed out to your brother that I did not consider it sporting of me to take advantage of your father's ignorance regarding some of the paintings in the Castle which are not portraits of your ancestors."

Marista gave a little cry.

"How can . . . you be so . . . generous to . . . us?"

"Anthony is very satisfied with the arrangements, and I think you will find when you see him again that he is a very excited young man."

"See him . . . again?" Marista enquired. "Where is . . . he?"

"At the moment he is riding one of my horses. He has told me that it is a long time since he has had anything well trained and spirited to ride, so he intends to put in a lot of practice before he joins the Regiment."

"I know how . . . happy Anthony will be," Marista said, "and I do not know . . . how to . . . thank you."

"I will tell you how you can do that later," the Earl said, "but next we have to consider Letty."

"Letty?"

"My nephew Peregrine has asked her to marry him."

Marista made a little sound that was incoherent, and the Earl continued:

"I am well aware, Marista, that you thought Peregrine would return to London and break her heart, but I assure you he is very eloquent about what he wants. I have discussed this with my sister, and we were thinking of Letty rather than of Peregrine when we decided it would not do either of them any harm to wait."

"You do not wish them to be . . . married?" Marista asked.

"Not immediately," the Earl replied. "Letty is, I understand, not yet eighteen, and Peregrine is only three years older. My sister agrees that it would be a good idea for her to take Letty with her to London and introduce her to the *Beau Monde*."

Marista clasped her hands together and the Earl continued:

"If the two young people have an understanding between themselves, it is to be kept secret, so that if either of them changes their mind before Christmas, then they are at liberty to do so. Otherwise, their engagement will be announced and they can be married in the New Year."

"It sounds . . . too . . . too . . . wonderful!" Marista cried. "And I know . . . that is what Mama would want . . . because living here, Letty knows so few young men."

"Actually, I was thinking it would be what you wanted," the Earl said.

Marista hesitated before she said in a worried little voice:

"But Letty will . . . require gowns and . . . many other things if she is to be in . . . London, and as you know . . . we cannot . . . afford them."

"I think," the Earl said with a note of laughter in his voice, "that this is where we have to bend your Rockbourne pride a little. If you cannot afford to give Letty gowns, I certainly could not have afforded last night to be murdered while I slept. You saved me, Marista, and I am in your debt."

"I do not . . . want you to . . . think of it like that," Marista said quickly. "As you are aware that man should not have been in England, but he paid . . . Anthony such an . . . enormous amount of money to be . . . brought here."

"I believe he would not only have offered him money," the Earl said quietly. "If he had refused, Anthony might have been forced into doing what he wanted."

Marista gave a little cry of horror.

"You . . . mean he . . . threatened him?"

"I do not think he did so, because Anthony was amenable," the Earl replied, "but I have heard how these French spies terrorise the smugglers into bringing them into this country, and it is dangerous to expect mercy from a man like that."

"It is horrible . . . beastly to . . . think about."

"Then forget it," the Earl answered. "You saved me, and Tolmarsh is dead, and I have agreed with Anthony that from this moment we shall all forget that he even existed."

"I will . . . try to do . . . so," Marista said meekly.

"Now, let me see . . ." the Earl said. "I have told you about Anthony and Letty. What else was there?"

Marista waited, her heart beating so violently that she was afraid he might hear it.

Then, as she hoped he would say that she could continue to live in Dovecot House without paying rent, he went on:

"Yes, of course, the Estate! I have already seen my

Manager and the Agents who will be in charge here, and I have told them to take on many more labourers in every department, preferably those who were employed here during your father's time. The farms are being repaired and so are the cottages, and the pensioners in them will have their money raised."

It was exactly what her father would have wished, and the way he spoke brought tears to Marista's eyes.

"How can . . . you be so . . . wonderful?" she said in a broken voice.

Then suddenly, without even thinking about it, she moved from the chair to cross the hearth-rug, and knelt beside him.

"I was . . . ready to go down on . . . my knees and . . . plead with you to . . . help us," she said, "but now I want to kneel and . . . thank you . . . and to say . . . over and over again . . . thank you . . . thank you!"

She spoke with such intensity that the tears overflowed from her eyes and ran down her cheeks.

The Earl was looking at her, but he did not touch her and merely said:

"I have not quite finished what I was telling you, Marista."

"I . . . I am . . . sorry," she murmured.

"I was only going to say that when the improvements are all made and the Estate is prosperous, I thought that when the time comes we could give it to the seventh Baronet as a wedding-present."

For a moment Marista found it impossible to understand what he had said.

As she stared at him, his face was misty because of her tears, and yet at the same time she was vividly conscious that his eyes held hers and she could not look away.

"I said 'we,' " the Earl said. "Did you hear me?"

155

"I . . . I do not . . . understand," Marista whispered.

"Then perhaps I can explain more eloquently without words," he said.

He put out his hands and lifted her against him, holding her so that she was half-sitting, half-lying in his arms.

Then as she gave a little gasp, his lips came down on hers, holding her captive.

He kissed her until she felt as she had last night, that he carried her into the sky and once again he was part of everything she loved and it was all beautiful and perfect because he was there.

He kissed her until she felt he gave her the shimmering gold of the sea and the sun. The shafts of sunlight seemed to run through her body, bringing her an ecstasy she had never known, so poignant, so rapturous, that she felt she was no longer on earth.

Only when the Earl raised his head did she look up at him and say in a voice that did not seem to be her own:

"I . . . love you! I did not . . . know that . . . love could be so utterly . . . completely . . . wonderful!"

"Nor did I," the Earl replied, then he was kissing her again.

Only after a century of wonder and glory, while Marista felt as if her whole body was vibrating with feelings that she had no idea even existed, did she lay her head against his shoulder to say:

"How can . . . you be so . . . marvellous and so . . . different from . . . what we . . . expected?"

"You have bewitched me," he replied. "Or perhaps the right word is 'enchanted.' I had no idea that any woman could make me feel as you do."

Marista raised her face to look up at him.

"Is that . . . true?"

"Ever since I have known you," the Earl said, "I have found your face haunting me, and I have been unable to think of anything but you."

"What are you . . . saying?" Marista asked. "Can it be . . . true?"

"It is true," he replied. "But how could I have guessed, how could I have imagined for one moment that when I brought my sister here to the Castle to convalesce, I would find the two things I have been looking for all my life."

"What were they?"

"You! And Love! I thought the perfect woman would always elude me, and also the emotion that other people have eulogised over, which I had never felt."

"How . . . can *that* be . . . true?"

"I am speaking of love, which is very different from desire," the Earl said.

He felt that she did not understand, and he said:

"I will not pretend to you, my lovely one, that there have not been a great many women in my life, and I know my reputation has preceded me, which is why you expected there to be orgies at the Castle."

Marista blushed and hid her face against him.

"Forgive . . . me," she murmured.

"It is quite understandable," the Earl replied, "and I am sure many of the parties which I have given could compare quite favourably with those given by the Romans, and were doubtless far more enjoyable."

His arms tightened before he said:

"When I saw you, I knew that even though you were hating me, you were everything in life I wanted, although I had no idea you even existed."

"How . . . could you have . . . thought that?"

"I think we are both aware that our intuition works rather better and certainly more truthfully than our brains."

"That is true," Marista agreed, "and yet I cannot think . . . now why I . . . hated you instead of . . . realising how . . . wonderful you . . . are."

"If I am wonderful it is because you have made me so," the Earl replied. "At the same time, you are far too beautiful for me to take any chances of losing you. How soon will you marry me?"

He felt Marista quiver at the words. Then she said:

"Are you quite . . . sure that is . . . something you . . . should do? I might . . . disappoint you as a . . . wife."

"Are you really suggesting that I should go back to London and leave you here?" the Earl asked.

Instinctively Marista put out her hand to hold on to the lapel of his coat, as if she was afraid he was already going. Then she said:

"I was thinking this morning that when you . . . left, it would be an indescribable agony . . . and I would never . . . love anybody . . . again. But it would be worse if I . . . disappointed you and you were . . . ashamed of me."

"That is like asking me if I would be ashamed of the flowers in the garden or the sunshine on the sea," the Earl said. "Everything I have seen about you so far, Marista, has been perfect, and I have yet to find a flaw."

"Then, please . . . please . . . do not look too hard! At the . . . same time . . ."

She paused, and the Earl said quietly:

"Go on!"

"I am . . . afraid of being your . . . wife," she whispered, "because you are of such . . . importance in the . . . Social World."

She thought he did not understand, and she said quickly:

"I love and adore you as a . . . man. You are . . .

158

everything I have always . . . dreamt a man should
be: strong . . . authoritative, and at the same time
more kind and understanding than I ever believed any
. . . man could be."

The Earl's lips were against her forehead, but he
did not speak, and after a moment she said:

"But . . . I will not be marrying you . . . but the
Earl of Stanbrook, who is of such . . . social importance . . . and who, as Papa said . . . is a challenge!
Supposing I cannot . . . live up to . . . him, and I am a
. . . failure?"

The Earl held her so closely against him that she
could hardly breathe before he said:

"Do you suppose I will not look after you, protect
you, and make sure you do not make any mistakes? You
are mine, Marista, mine completely and absolutely, and
when you are my wife, I will love, adore, and worship
you for the rest of my life."

"Are you . . . really saying this to . . . me?" she
asked. "I feel I must be . . . dreaming, or else it is
. . . part of my . . . imagination."

"It is only the beginning of the things I am going to
say to you," the Earl said, "and let me assure you, I am
very much surprised by my own eloquence."

Because Marista knew that he was mocking his own
feelings and yet very much aware of them, she put up
her hand to touch his cheek.

"Are you absolutely certain that you want me?" she
asked. "I love you until I would rather . . . die than do
anything to harm or hurt you in any way."

There was a throb in her voice as she went on:

"Last night when I thought . . . you might be
killed, I suffered an agony that was more . . . painful
than anything I have ever . . . felt in my . . . whole
life, and it is that same . . . agony I would feel if
I . . . failed you in . . . any way."

"You will not fail me," the Earl said, "and, my darling, because I understand what you are trying to say to me, I know we have been more blessed than any two people ever have been in finding each other."

He did not wait for her to answer, but kissed her until it was impossible to think, but only to feel that she was already his and nothing and nobody could divide them.

"I love you! I love you!" she wanted to cry.

But her lips were saying it for her, and her heart was beating to the same words, and the sunshine coming through the window was a blessing from God.

"I love you! I love you!"

The words seemed to rise from them both like a paean of wonder towards the sky.

*     *     *

Marista and the Earl stood on the steps of the Castle to watch the carriages moving away down the drive.

The first one held Lady Lampton and Letty, and was drawn by four of the Earl's superlative horses. In the second were Anthony and Peregrine.

Marista knew they would easily reach their destination by five o'clock as planned.

They were staying the night with a friend of the Earl's who lived not far off the Dover Road, and tomorrow they would be in London, where Letty, wildly excited at the idea, was to be provided with a wardrobe of clothes in which to be presented to the fashionable world by Lady Lampton.

"It is so thrilling!" Letty said over and over again. "I do not know if I am on my head or my heels! But I love Peregrine and he loves me, and however long we have to wait, we shall still love each other and no-one else."

Marista thought this was very likely true. At the

same time, she could understand why the Earl had thought it right that Letty should have a chance to meet other men in case her love for Peregrine was just a passing infatuation.

Because she wanted to tease him, she had said:

"I cannot quite . . . understand why you think Letty might . . . change her mind and not . . . me."

The Earl put his fingers under her chin and turned her face up to his.

"Is that what you want to do?"

Because it was impossible not to tell him the truth, she answered:

"I know that if . . . every man in the world . . . laid his . . . heart at my . . . feet, it would not make the slightest . . . difference to what I . . . feel for . . . you."

"Or I for you," the Earl answered. "But if you think I would risk losing you, then you are very much mistaken. You are mine, Marista, and as I am extremely jealous, as I always will be, I do not intend to allow you to see any other man until you are my wife."

It was of course the Earl who arranged everything, and although Marista was only too happy to do anything he wished, she found herself almost breathless with the way in which he set the wheels in motion.

Anything he wanted took place as if by the wave of a magic wand.

Because he felt she would like it he told Marista that they would be married in the little Norman Church where she had been christened, and where the tombs of the Rockbournes decorated every wall.

"I want nobody there."

"But will your friends not think it strange?" Marista asked.

"I will have nobody there but you and your family," he replied. "My relations, of whom there are a large number, will be represented by my sister and Peregrine."

His determination swept away Marista's fear of meeting the fashionable world and what she was sure would be his critical friends before she had become his wife.

As if he understood, he said:

"You know that I want you entirely to myself, and because it seems somehow appropriate, I can think of no place as attractive as the Castle to start our honeymoon. We will go on later to one of my houses in another part of England, which I am waiting to show you."

"It would be . . . marvellous beyond words to . . . honeymoon at the . . . Castle."

As she spoke, Marista felt that because he had been so wonderful and had promised that he would return the Estate eventually to Anthony, her father and mother would bless them.

And so would the Rockbourne ancestors looking down from their gold frames and approving the renovations which the Earl had already made to the Castle, and of which he told Marista there were to be many more.

Because it was all for Anthony, she was more touched than she could say, but it was easier to kiss the Earl than to put it into words.

Because her lips were very soft, sweet, and innocent, her kisses were very different from those he had received in the past.

Yet he was aware that she aroused a desire in him that was not only a blazing fire but also a spiritual experience which he had never known before.

Being very intelligent, the Earl realised that what he felt for Marista was the idealistic love he had believed in when he was young, but had lost when he entered the bored, cynical Social World in which he had become an acknowledged leader.

The chivalry which had lain dormant until now made him want to protect her not only from other men who would frighten her, like Dashford, but also from himself.

Because her innocence and purity enveloped her like the moonlight through which she had come to save him from being murdered, he knew that she was in a shrine in his heart which had always lain empty until now.

When he had said he worshipped her, it was really true.

He was already planning that they would live a very different life from what he had lived in the past, and his riotous parties, like his riotous friends, would all be forgotten.

They would entertain at his ancestral home in Buckinghamshire, and in the years ahead they would make it a place of happiness not only for themselves but for their children.

He knew that Marista would love his horses as he did and would be thrilled when they won their races.

She would also be happy when they rode together over the land which he owned, and he was certain that she would become somebody to be respected and loved, to whom his tenants, his pensioners, and his employees would turn in times of trouble.

"I love her!" the Earl said to himself as he lay alone in the big canopied bed to which she had come through the secret door to save him.

"I love her, and because I will be very gentle and tender towards her, our love will increase with the years until I shall become a model of respectability and propriety."

He was laughing at himself, and yet at the same time it was something that he wanted to come true.

They were married early in the morning in the little Norman Church in the Park. While the villagers and the tenants waited outside to cheer them, inside there was nobody except for their families and of course Hannah.

Marista's gown, which he had ordered from London, was so exquisite that when she wore it she felt she was no longer herself but some mythical being that had come from the sea to live amongst human beings.

To the Earl she looked as she had when he had seen her enveloped in the moonlight, standing by his bed, and thought for one incredible moment that she was a vision.

After they were married by the old Rector the Earl had lifted her veil, and as she looked up at him shyly with her eyes filled with love, he had known that he dedicated himself to her service for as long as he should live.

Marista's face was radiant with happiness as they walked together down the aisle, and then they had all driven to the Castle for luncheon.

Anthony made an excellent speech, and the Earl replied wittily and amusingly, but still with an underlying sincerity which Marista understood and loved.

After the luncheon was over the carriages were waiting to take them to London, and Letty looked exquisitely lovely in a new gown and bonnet which had come from London with Marista's wedding-gown.

"Oh, dearest Marista," she said, "I cannot believe this is all happening to us after we were so depressed, so frightened that we would be turned out of Dovecot House and die of starvation."

Marista slipped her hand into her husband's as she answered:

"It was you, Letty, who told me to come and beg the Earl for . . . mercy."

Letty laughed.

"If this is mercy, I could do with a great deal more of it!"

"You are not to be greedy!" Marista admonished automatically, and Letty laughed again.

"There is no harm in asking," she replied.

Then she kissed the Earl and said:

"Thank you, thank you! Nobody could have a more generous or marvellous brother-in-law than you. The only mistake I made was in not coming to the Castle myself instead of sending Marista!"

"You are a minx!" the Earl replied, his eyes twinkling. "I only hope that Peregrine is strong enough to keep you in order."

"If she behaves badly," Peregrine replied, "I shall bring her back here and lock her in the dungeons at the bottom of the Norman Tower until she behaves herself."

"You are frightening me!" Letty protested mockingly, and Peregrine said:

"You will find out that I mean what I say if when I get to London you try any tricks!"

Although they were teasing each other, Marista saw so much love in their eyes that she was certain Letty had found the man with whom she could be happy for the rest of her life.

It was not quite the same, she thought, as what she and the Earl felt for each other, but it would develop with the years.

In the meantime, they were very young, and if they wanted to dance and laugh and not be too serious, then it was exactly as it should be.

"Good-bye, Anthony," the Earl was saying. "I have written to the Colonel, who is an old friend of mine, and I think when you present yourself at the Barracks tomorrow morning you will find he will welcome you."

"I have no idea how to thank you," Anthony answered, "but look after Marista. She deserves every-

thing you have given her, because it was she who kept
our spirits high during the bad times."

"I will look after her," the Earl promised.

Marista knew it was a vow that he had already
made while they were being married.

They both waved until the carriages were out of
sight, then hand-in-hand they walked back into the
Castle together.

"I must go take off my wedding-gown," Marista
said.

The Earl did not reply, he only walked up the
stairs beside her, and when she would have gone to her
mother's room, which was now hers, he drew her into
the Master-Bedroom, where she had not been since she
had come through the secret panel.

It was just as impressive as she always remembered it, except that she saw the carpet was new and so
were the deep red velvet curtains.

They made a perfect background for the white
lilies which had been arranged in every corner of the
room and on some of the furniture.

She was surprised to see them, and as she looked
enquiringly at the Earl, he said:

"It was here in this room, my darling, that I first
knew you loved me as I loved you."

"You mean . . . you really knew it when you . . .
kissed me?"

"I knew when I touched your lips that you gave me
your heart," he replied, "and that we were no longer
two people but one."

"But you . . . loved me before . . . that?"

"I loved you, but I thought you still hated me as
you told me you did, and I was afraid I might never be
able to make you love me."

As he spoke he put his arms round her, then he
said:

"When I kissed you and it was more wonderful than any kiss I had ever given or received, I reached for you across Eternity and I knew we were meant for each other. Even when we die we will not be separated."

"I feel that too," Marista said, "and now I love you so . . . much that the whole world is full of . . . love because . . . you are there. I feel I am dreaming . . . and it cannot be . . . true that I am yours . . . and I am your wife."

"I will make you believe it," the Earl said very tenderly.

As he spoke he lifted the wreath of orange-blossoms from her head and took off the gossamer-fine lace veil which had been worn by Rockbourne brides for generations.

He looked at her in her soft white gown and thought it would be impossible for any other woman to be so exquisitely lovely and at the same time so innocent and untouched.

She was like a magnolia blossom in bud, he thought, and he knew this was what he had always wanted but thought he would never find.

Very gently he put his arms round her and pulled her close against him.

"I love you, my adorable wife," he said, "but I have no wish to frighten you or shock you in any way. If I ever see the hatred in your eyes which was there when we first met, I think I would want to kill myself!"

Marista gave a little cry of protest. Then she said:

"How could you say . . . anything like . . . that? I love you . . . and you could never . . . shock me. I am yours . . . completely and absolutely . . . yours."

There was a note in her voice which had never been there before, and as she lifted her lips to his and the Earl kissed her, he knew that he was awakening a little flame within her.

He held her closer and still closer, and as he felt as

if her body melted into his and her heart was beating wildly, he very gently undid her wedding-gown.

It fell to the floor, and, still holding her lips captive, he lifted her onto the great bed in which the Rockbournes had lived and loved, been born and died, and lived again.

Then as the Earl joined her and Marista felt the hard strength of his body against the softness of hers, she felt not only as if they were surrounded by love and the blessings of past generations, but that the sunshine outside was bringing them a Divine message from God.

It was the message of love, the love that the Earl was giving her and which she wanted to give him.

The love that was the act of giving and was an ecstasy that came not only from the body and the heart but also from the soul.

As the Earl drew her closer and still closer, his kisses awakened in her strange sensations she had never known, and her body seemed to move in unison with his, to the music which came from the sky and the sound of the sea.

Then as he made her his, she knew that not only were their bodies united but also their souls.

This was love in all its glory, the love which would survive not only life but death and was theirs for all Eternity.